Praise for
Rusty and Emma's Big Shock

"This delightful story with its gorgeous illustrations begins when Rusty, an old dog, Emma Puff, a 90-year-old woman, and Mr. Musk, the parrot, go into the woods to find plants for Emma's medicines. One day, they find strange purple seed spheres that Emma cooks in her Magic Cooking Pot. Then the fun begins! The story has all the elements kids enjoy like poo and food fights, and the story has twists and turns that will delight young readers."

—**Mickey Goodman**, co-author of
The Cowboy Little, Cowboy Small Series

"A beautifully magical story for all readers. Sure to be cherished. Emma and Rusty's tale will captivate audiences from the first page."

—**Jennifer Gillman**, owner of The Book Exchange, Marietta, Georgia

"The story was interesting and funny. I loved the illustrations, because they had a watercolor texture. My favorite characters are Emma and her dog Rusty. I was surprised that George had red hair when he was a child. I loved the book!"

—**Gracy Issa**, age nine

D1160862

EMMA PUFF'S SECRETS SERIES | BOOK 1

RUSTY AND EMMA'S
BIG SHOCK!

STORY BY ANNIE WILDE
ILLUSTRATIONS BY BEEBE HARGROVE

LUCID
HOUSE
PUBLISHING

LU☾ID
HOUSE
PUBLISHING

Published in the United States by Lucid House Publishing, LLC, Marietta, Georgia
www.LucidHousePublishing.com
Copyright ©Annie Wilde 2023
Illustrations Copyright ©Beebe Hargrove 2023
First Edition. All rights reserved.
This title is available in print and e-book form via Lucid House Publishing, LLC as well as an audiobook in partnership with Blackstone Publishing.
Cover and interior design: The Design Lab Atlanta, Inc.
Author's photo: Larry Scaggs Illustrator's photo: Russ Hargrove

This book is a work of fiction. Any references in this book to real people, or places are used fictitiously. Other names, characters, places, and events are products of the author's wild imagination, and any resemblance to actual events, places, or persons, living or dead, is entirely coincidental. Please note that the story is set in England and includes a glossary of words (some with United Kingdom English spelling) that may be unfamiliar and appear in italics.

Library of Congress Cataloging-in-Publication Data
Annie Wilde, 1948-
Rusty and Emma's big shock!/ book 1 of Emma Puff's secrets series
/Wilde, Annie –1st U.S. edition
Hargrove, Beebe, 1981-
Library of Congress Control Number: TK
Print ISBN 978-1950495412
E-book ISBN 978-1950495429

1. fantasy and magic 2. action and adventure 3. England 4. talking parrot
5. ageism 6. diversity 7. orphans and foster homes 8. rescue dog 9. Christmas

JUV037000, JUV013050, JUV001000, JUV017010, JUV045000

Dedication

A huge thank you to my partner Doug,

my daughters and my granddaughter. Also to

my amazing friends who have all supported me

throughout this fun project that has lived in

my head for many years!

A special lady named Marcia gave me the

encouragement to put Emma Puff on paper.

The child is in us all forever, believe,

and the magic begins.

Contents

Introduction: Rusty and the Secrets 1
Chapter 1: Crazy Happenings in the Woods 3
Chapter 2: Mr. Musk Makes Adjustments. 9
Chapter 3: How Old Are We?. 13
Chapter 4: Chocolate and Lies. 19
Chapter 5: Nothing to Wear 23
Chapter 6: Who Might You Be? 27
Chapter 7: Tin Lizzie Gets Cranked 31
Chapter 8: Let's Go Down to the River. 37
Chapter 9: I Dare You 43
Chapter 10: Buses, Banks, and Bold Emma 47
Chapter 11: Money, Please 51
Chapter 12: Burgers and BrightPink Wool 55
Chapter 13: Meet Mr. Musk. 61
Chapter 14: So Much Fun, So Much Mess. 67
Chapter 15: Mr. Doshmore Gets a Shock 73
Chapter 16: Big Driving Shoes 81
Chapter 17: Stop the Car! 85
Chapter 18: No, Emma! No! 91
Chapter 19: Where Is Old Emma Puff? 97
Chapter 20: Policemen Everywhere 101
Chapter 21: Time to Say Goodbye 105
Chapter 22: The Wonderful Goldhearts. 109
Chapter 23: Christmas Is Coming 113
Chapter 24: Snow-Covered Boots. 117
Glossary 122
Emma Puff's Secrets Book Club Questions 125
About the Author. 129
About the Illustrator 130

Rusty and the Secrets

*D*id you open this book because you like secrets?

I love to be told a secret, but as hard as I try, I just can't keep them to myself. That is why I'm about to tell you a big one!

My name is Rusty. I think I'm a very cute puppy. I'm sensible with a big personality. But I used to be a very scruffy, old, grumpy dog with issues.

My owner, Emma Puff, is a pretty young girl. She tells a lot of lies and does the craziest things and that's because only a few days ago, Emma was a ninety-year-old lady. She was often cranky, sometimes crazy, and always a little outrageous! Ninety years is probably older than your great-grandparents.

You might be thinking, this doesn't make any sense. Please bear with me, all will be revealed.

When Emma and I were both old, we didn't live with Tom and Jemma Goldheart, who, by the way, are the nicest people on the planet. We didn't live in this huge posh house with its plush carpets, paintings on the walls, cosy log fires and the biggest Christmas tree ever.

Yes, it's Christmas Eve. Emma and I are both very excited.

Emma asked me before she went to bed not to bark at the man with a big white beard, wearing a red suit and hat, and carrying a sack of presents. She said he would probably say, "HO, HO, HO." She also said he leaves presents under the Christmas tree for children who haven't been naughty.

Are you kidding me? All children are naughty sometimes.

Emma and I only arrived here yesterday and to be honest, I'm so glad we did. Since Emma has been young again, she's been up to all sorts of unbelievable stuff. Just a few days ago, when we were both very old, we lived in a creaky, leaky, draughty old cottage in the middle of the woods. The windows rattled, the roof leaked, and the wind blew in under the doors. The place was falling down, and it stank of parrot poop. Mr. Musk, Emma's annoying parrot, made sure of that.

Mr. Musk talks a lot. He doesn't know what he's saying. He just repeats everything he hears, over and over and OVER again. Sometimes he gets all the words muddled up. He's also very mischievous, and it's because of his mischief that I have this story to tell.

It all began a little while ago. I had just woken up...

CHAPTER 1

Crazy Happenings in the Woods

"RUSTY!" Emma screeched at me, in her croaky voice. "We're going to the woods. Now where's my hat? Have you eaten my hat? You pesky dog."

She mumbled to herself and glared at me as she emptied out the closet, tossing an assortment of random items onto the floor.

Emma never threw anything away. "This may come in handy," was one of her most used phrases.

"PESKY DOG, PESKY DOG, WHERE'S MY HAT, WHERE'S MY HAT," squawked Mr. Musk, as he bobbed his bright yellow head up and down, whilst perched on top of the kitchen curtain pole.

There were no curtains hanging on the pole. Emma had thrown them away as they were covered in parrot poop. She would never ask Mr. Musk to stay in his cage during the day, only at bedtime, when she would drape a large red blanket over the top of it. The blanket worked like magic because he instantly stopped talking, much to my relief.

"Be quiet, Mr. Musk. Pesky parrot," said Emma, placing her hat on her wispy white hair. She had found her hat exactly where she had left it, on the hat stand.

She grabbed her stick and picked up her basket. Mr. Musk flew down and positioned himself comfortably on her right shoulder. He always came along for a walk in the woods. He'd never fly away. Sometimes I wish he would.

As I watched Emma hobbling along the path, I wondered if she knew she was wearing odd socks. One green and one brown, pulled up to her knobbly, crinkly knees from her scruffy, hiking boots which were coming apart at the seams.

Her wispy white hair was sticking out from under her flamboyant red hat, which she'd picked up at a jumble sale. She said she loved the feathers on it, and there were plenty of them flopping all over the place, together with huge dried flowers and sparkly things. I'm sure it was once used in a carnival.

You could hardly see her face, apart from her glasses that were held together with bright pink wool and perched on the end of her wrinkly nose. She had very few teeth and constantly looked like she was chewing something.

Her coat was a faded blue colour, with an assortment of odd buttons. She replaced them year after year, and the her sleeves had been repaired with the same bright pink wool many times. The back of her coat was decorated with parrot mess.

We went to the woods every day, without fail, whatever the weather. The walking did wonders for Emma's health and connecting with nature was great for her soul. However, the real reason had nothing to do with Emma's well-being at all, but rather her love of animals.

She gathered healing plants and berries that grew there and used them to make magic medicines for all the animals in her village and beyond. All the animals (the wild ones and the ones with owners) loved Emma and appreciated her magic healing potions.

But this day was no ordinary day. It turned out to be an extremely extraordinary day.

I wandered off sniffing around in all my favorite places, darting in and out of the trees. Us dogs can tell a lot by a smell. Did you know that?

Mr. Musk perched on the branch of a tree next to Emma. A lot of birds were singing and whistling in the trees and, try as he might, he just could not do either. He can talk, but he certainly cannot whistle, and his singing voice is terrible. It's so funny listening to his squeaky squawks.

I was tracking the scent of a young rabbit who'd been dodging me for weeks. He owed me an apology for covering me in dirt when he was digging his burrow.

Suddenly, something knocked me off my paws backwards, then something knocked me sideways. I was being punched and thrown all over the place. Huge, glowing purple spheres, covered in what looked like sunflower seeds, were springing up out of the ground with enough force to knock over a tree. I'd never seen anything like them, and they just kept coming. Pop! Pop! Pop!

I totally freaked out as another one sent me hurtling over a bush and landing on my head.

"Oh my, just look at these!" gasped Emma. "Have you ever? I have never," she mumbled as she inspected the spheres more closely. She was so busy poking, prodding, and sniffing the strange purple balls that she never even asked me if my head was hurting.

"Oh my! Oh my! Just look at these!" echoed Mr. Musk.

"Come on, Rusty," Emma shouted, her basket brimming over with enormous purple spheres, another tucked under her arm. "I've got to get these home and find out if they're poisonous."

The parrot was now back on Emma's shoulder, looking at me, "Poisonous, Rusty! Come on, Rusty!"

There are a lot of strange plants and berries that grow in the woods. Many of them are poisonous, even those that look delicious, so unless you're a foraging expert like Emma, you must never eat them.

As we followed the path that led out of the woods, I glanced back to take another look at the giant offending things, but they had all disappeared.

CHAPTER 2

Mr. Musk Makes Adjustments

$\mathcal{A}$s soon as we arrived home, a very excited Emma, carrying her basket of strange round purple seed spheres, went straight into her cabin and locked the door.

Her cabin was where she prepared all the wonderful medicines, and I was not allowed in. I peeped in once and saw jars of every size, some full, some empty, and a huge cooking pot and shelves filled with books.

Mr. Musk had decided to sit in my basket. I stared at him, showed him my front teeth and did my best growl. He didn't care. He just carried on preening his bright blue feathers with his glossy red beak. He is without doubt a very handsome bird, but unfortunately, without manners.

I was starving and it was way past my dinner time. Emma had been out in her cabin for hours.

At long last Emma entered the kitchen carrying what she called her Magic Cooking Pot. I could see it was full of the strange purple things. She carefully placed the huge pot onto the grubby cast iron range cooker and began to cook them.

"These are not poisonous, Rusty," she said, looking straight at me. "I don't know what they are or how or why they popped up like they did. But I have a very good feeling about them, a very good feeling indeed."

"Popped up! Good feeling! Poisonous Rusty!" continued the parrot, as he landed on Emma's shoulder, dipping his head and staring at me. I showed him my teeth. No reaction this time either.

I really wanted my dinner and just as Emma reached to open the cupboard there was a knock at the door.

"Only me," said the gruff voice of George Cracknall, Emma's best friend, as he stepped into the kitchen holding a box.

As usual, George removed his cap and his boots, and, as always, his toes were peeping through his ancient black wool socks. His torn trousers were covered in mud and instead of using a belt, he'd tied them up with rope that sat snugly under his protruding belly. His cheeks were always very rosy and his bulbous nose constantly runny, so he wiped it frequently with his large grubby handkerchief. I'm sure this was the reason why he had a very large bushy grey moustache under it.

He was a very generous man with a heart of gold. He loved animals, especially me, and always fussed and greeted me with a treat that he pulled from his pocket.

When I was just a little bit older than I am now, when I was a puppy the first time, George saved my life. My previous owner was a very cruel man. He kept me tied up with rope to a tree. He beat me with a stick and only fed me scraps of bread once a week. I chewed and chewed on the rope until it broke free. Then I ran and hid under a bush. That's where George found me and brought me to Emma.

"I've brought you some turnips and carrots, Emma. Grew 'em me self," he said, wiping his nose.

Mr. Musk chirped in from the curtain pole, "Grew 'em me self! Grew 'em me self! Grew 'em me self!"

Then with a big smile George said, "Can't get fresher than these beauties. You can make yerself a nice soup. There's a big storm coming tonight, and you know my knees have been hurting, so I'll not be stopping by later, my dear. But I will pop round tomorrow."

He paused and huffed as he pulled on his boots, "Oh, and by the way, them there city folks have been back again. Left a terrible mess they did. Took me an hour to pick it all up. Come 'ere for them picnics. Leave all their rubbish, plastic bags, glass bottles, and not a thought for the animals."

And then, closing the door, he was gone.

Emma tutted, smiled, and rolled her eyes, then set about making soup with the vegetables George had brought.

Once the soup was simmering on the range, Emma gave Mr. Musk the end of the wooden spoon to hold in his beak and stir. She often did this. At least it kept him quiet.

I settled into my basket and kept an eye on the mischievous bird.

Mr. Musk sat silently on the trivet hanging above the range, gently stirring the soup.

He then decided that the other pot on the range, Emma's magic one, the one full of the unknown purple spheres, could also do with some stirring. He also decided that as one pot was much fuller than the other pot, he would make some adjustments...

CHAPTER 3

How Old Are We?

*N*ormally I don't like soup, but this soup was delicious. Emma had added a little to my dinner, so whatever Mr. Musk did to it, the soup had my approval. After a second helping, I was stuffed and ready for my basket.

Following a quick visit to the garden, where the wind, rain, and distant thunder made me shiver, I hurried back into the cottage. Emma opened the door wearing her long pink nightdress and a matching knitted wool hat with a plastic bag tied over it that she said she needed to keep her warm and dry because the roof leaked. "George was certainly right about a storm coming, Rusty, I think it's going to be a big one."

Then she locked the door, placed the red blanket over Musk's cage, turned off the light, and said goodnight. I snuggled down in my basket.

The crashing thunder and crackling lightning awoke me. I felt cold and was bursting to visit the garden. Most unusual for me but even stranger was the fact that I couldn't climb out of my basket. It had gotten bigger.

The wind was howling, the windows were rattling, and it was very dark. At first, I thought maybe I was dreaming, but no. My need to piddle was very real. I tried to jump out of my giant basket and 'DONK!', I jumped headfirst into a huge rock. A dazed and confused me fell back. I knew I had a small bone in my basket, but not a rock.

Suddenly, the room filled with light, and I was being lifted up by a beautiful young girl. She had long brown hair, lots of freckles, and very white teeth. As if I wasn't already confused enough, she was wearing Emma's nightdress, holding the hem up, as it was far too long.

"Rusty!" she squealed holding me up high.

"Rusty! It's me, Emma! Look at me. Look at you. Look at us. We're young again," I heard her little voice say.

"I'm busting to piddle." It was my voice. I was talking.

"Who was that?" Emma asked, putting me down on the rug. "Rusty, did you just talk, or am I hearing things?"

"I'm busting to piddle," I said urgently.

"Rusty, did you just say, 'I'm busting to piddle?'"

"I did."

"Goodness," gasped Emma. "I can hear you. Oh, my! That's incredible. Whatever has happened to us?"

"Can I go piddle?" I repeated.

"I can't believe it, we're young, and I can hear you. You're talking. You said, 'Can I go piddle?'"

"I did. I'm busting, Emma."

"You just said my name. You said 'Emma.' This is impossible."

"I did," I said, while my eyes watered and all four legs were crossed.

"This is so exciting!" she squealed. "Maybe I'm dreaming. This cannot be real. When I went to bed, I was ninety years old."

Emma knelt down next to me and stroked my ears. "You were an old dog, and now you're a puppy who can talk. Say something else, Rusty."

I looked up at her, feeling awkward and said, "I've just piddled on the rug."

"Oh, Rusty, I'm sorry. This is my fault. I was just so shocked that you are talking, and we're young. I can't believe it. I keep pinching myself to wake up. I must be dreaming. Are we really young again?" She stretched her back and lifted her arms up high. "I feel amazing. I've got no achy, creaky bones."

Then, staring in the mirror, she said with a big toothy smile, "And I've got all my teeth back, and look at my long brown hair and my face, no wrinkles. I can see clearly and hear everything."

Then looking at me, she asked, "How about you, Rusty? How do you feel?"

"Erm. I feel small and erm, my stiff back legs don't hurt anymore and erm, I'm hungry." I tried to smile, but that was difficult. Turns out my smile and my growl are pretty similar.

"I'm hungry, too. I want to eat waffles with loads of syrup, chocolate cake, and apple pie."

Emma threw the rug out of the back door, twirled around the room, stared in the mirror, stuck out her tongue, examined her teeth, lifted her nightdress, wiggled her toes, stroked her long silky hair, did a handstand up against the wall and a cartwheel down the hallway. Running into the kitchen laughing she yelled, "Come on, Rusty, let's eat everything!"

CHAPTER 4

Chocolate and Lies

"Chocolate, yum! Yummy yum! I've got all my teeth," squawked Mr. Musk, positioning himself on the edge of the kitchen table, which was laden with an amazing assortment of half-eaten sweet gooey treats.

"I've got all my whaaa! Whaa!" he squawked, peering at Emma and ruffling his blue feathers.

"Oh dear, you don't know who I am do you, Mr. Musk?" she asked licking chocolate cream from her fingers. "I'm Emma. Yes, it's me. I know I look different and sound different. But it is me, I promise."

She offered him a slice of apple, which he took in his claw and nibbled. "I have a feeling that you, Mr. Musk, might just have something to do with why Rusty and I aren't old anymore."

I looked up at Emma and said, "He does. It was him. I saw him. He was mixing and messing with the cooking pots."

"I thought as much." said Emma.

"He mixed some of the soup with the mysterious purple seed spheres. Hah!" I said showing my teeth at him. "He might have killed us, Emma. He's always doing stupid things. And when you're not looking, he poops on my head, and you know he's always pooping in my basket. He should be kept in his cage."

"Oh dear, Rusty, you are upset with him, but now that you can talk, you can ask him directly not to do those things to you anymore," she said, busy admiring her new youthful self in the mirror.

I walked over to the table, looked Mr. Musk in the eyes, and said, "Please, no more pooping on me or my basket." He didn't even blink, so I shouted, "No more pooping!"

Still no reaction from him. It was like he couldn't hear me. I then shouted as loud as I could, with my eyes fixed on his. "Stupid parrot!" But nothing, no reaction whatsoever.

"Emma," I said, "I don't think he can hear what I'm saying. Maybe only you can hear me and no one else?"

Emma picked me up and said, "Maybe you're right, Rusty, maybe it is only me that can hear you. We'll have to test this out on George."

"Maybe George! Rusty right! Test! Test George maybe!" he screeched. Unfortunately, I could definitely still hear him.

"Sweet Rusty," she said stroking my ears, "I think you are between six to eight weeks old now, but with a wise old head." she giggled.

Then, looking back at the mirror, she asked, "How old am I? One thing's for sure, I'm not ninety anymore."

Emma stared at herself making a lot of different faces, smiling, frowning, mouth open, mouth shut, big toothy smile, lips pursed, tongue out, nose screwed up, and eventually she said "I think I'm about ten? Or maybe twelve? I might be nine? Or eight? Or even eleven? Oh, fiddle faddle. I haven't got a clue how old I am, but one thing's for sure: I look a sight fresher than I did yesterday."

"You're very pretty, Emma."

"Thank you, Rusty, but now I must think up a story about who I am and where the old Emma and old Rusty have gone. Whatever shall I say? I need to come up with a solid story and fast, and I'll have to get comfortable with telling a lot of lies."

"I'm sure you'll think of something, Emma. If we're staying young, then you will have to go back to school..."

"Oh gosh, no!" She huffed, stamping her foot and crossing her arms. I knew that look. Old Emma could be stubborn. Looked to me as if this young Emma was the same. "I certainly don't want to go to school again."

Then, looking up at Mr. Musk, who had returned to the curtain pole, her pout faded, and she said with a laugh, "It's a good thing you didn't have any soup last night, because I'm pretty sure, this morning you would have woken up as an egg."

"I wish," I laughed.

"Don't be mean, Rusty."

Mr. Musk squawked and garbled Emma's words, "Good thing! Good egg! Go to school! School! Don't be mean, Rusty!"

CHAPTER 5

Nothing to Wear

The air was fresh and smelt so good after last night's storm. Everything in the garden seemed so big now, and I was finding it difficult to do what I had to do.

As I walked into the kitchen I asked, "Emma, can you cut and trim the garden please? I'm having trouble doing what I have to do without something tickling my nose or prickling my bottom."

The kitchen looked like a herd of elephants had visited for breakfast. All the cupboards were flung open, flour all over the floor, open packets strewn everywhere, plates of half-eaten cakes piled on top of the dresser, and the sink was full of dirty bowls, pots, and pans.

In the middle of it all stood Emma with a pair of scissors in her hand, rummaging through a pile of her clothes sprawled all over the kitchen table.

"This place is a terrible mess, Emma. You should clean up in case George pops in."

"But I've got nothing to wear." she exclaimed, "And look."

She pointed to her shoes. "They're far too big. And all these horrible old clothes of mine which I've been wearing for years and years are all too big." She continued picking through the enormous pile.

"Do you think we'll stay young or will we go back to being old in the middle of the night?" I asked. "I mean, that is a possibility, isn't it? Or will we have to keep eating those strange purple balls forever?"

"Rusty," she said, waving her scissors at me. "I have a very good feeling that we are going to stay young and just grow old like we did before. Those purple spheres or balls or however you want to describe them, have the most amazing magical powers. Why they popped up like they did and disappeared again, I guess we will never know." Her eyes sparkled with mischief, and she smiled at the thought.

She rolled up pieces of newspaper and stuffed it into her shoes in an attempt to make them fit. "Once I have something to wear, I'm going down to the barn to have a look at my old car and see if it will start. Now that I can see and hear perfectly again, and my back doesn't hurt any more, we'll be able to go out for a nice drive."

"Emma! No, you can't do that." I exclaimed, jumping up at her. "Children do not drive cars."

"Oh, that's because they don't know how to drive, Rusty." she laughed. "But I do."

I climbed into my basket and curled up in a ball. No point in arguing with Emma Puff. I remembered the last time I was in her car. We nearly ended up in the river.

"How do I look, Rusty?" she asked as she hobbled around the kitchen wearing a purple skirt that she'd cut at least 20 centimeters off of, but it was still far too long. She'd tied pink wool around it to stop it from slipping off and paired it with a green wool sweater that she'd shrunk by mistake last summer. She'd accidentally boiled it in the washing machine with her sheets. However, it was still way too big.

I sized up her appearance. "I'm sorry Emma, but you look a total mess."

"Well, have you got any better ideas?" she said, glaring at me. "Look, the shoes will stay on if I curl up my toes." She walked awkwardly around the kitchen with pieces of torn up newspaper peeping out from them. Then came a familiar knock at the door.

"Hello Emma, it's me, George."

We both froze as we watched the creaky door slowly open. Emma whispered in my ear, "Rusty, don't talk, not a word."

"But I have to find out if he can hear me." I whispered back.

CHAPTER 6

Who Might You Be?

George Cracknall stood with his mouth wide open, clutching his handkerchief, as he slowly surveyed the chaos before him.

"Good Lord!" He exclaimed, stepping back and sending some dishes crashing off the dresser, grabbing it to steady himself. "What on earth has been going on in here!?"

"Wouldn't you like to know!" I said. He gave no reaction.

"Where is Emma? Emma!" George shouted. "Where are you?"

Then he focused his gaze on little Emma, scratched his head, wiped his nose, and asked, "And who might you be, young lady?"

"A fairy from the bottom of the garden," I said.

Still no reaction from George, just a glare from Emma.

"I'm Emma Puff's great niece," blurted Emma. "I'm her brother's granddaughter. I arrived late last night, and this is my puppy," she said, drawing in another deep breath, as she picked me up and passed me to George.

"His name is also Rusty. Aunt Emma told me you might pop in, but she had to go out this morning and doesn't know what time she'll be back."

Smiling sweetly, she added, "But may I make you a cup of tea?"

"Yes, have a nice cup of tea," I said.

George gently put me down. He most certainly could not hear me. He cleared some mess off a chair and sat down heavily upon it.

"Emma has never told me about any niece," he said, shaking his head. "Or a brother in all the years I have known her. Fancy that, a niece called Emma with a puppy called Rusty." He shook his head in disbelief again. "Well, I have never."

"Aunt! Well, I never! Well I never! Cup of tea!" parroted Mr. Musk.

George stood up, ignoring the bird. "Well, I'm pleased to meet you young Emma, but best you get this place cleaned up before your aunt returns, 'cause I don't think she'll be very 'appy when she sees this here mess."

He took a gulp of tea, pushed some clothes to the side so he could put his mug on the table and buttoned up his coat. "Be sure to tell her I popped in, and tell her I won't be around tomorrow, 'cause I'm finally seeing the doctor about my poor old achy knees."

"Yes, yes, I will." said Emma. "Nice to meet you too, Mr. Cracknall, and I hope your knees feel better soon."

She closed the door behind him and slumped down onto the floor.

"Phew, Rusty. I didn't expect George to come 'round so early, and you're right, he didn't hear you, so it seems only I can. I wonder how long he'll believe the story I've just told him. I do need to tell him everything, but not just yet."

"But Emma, he'll want to see the old you soon, so you'd better think of something quick," I warned.

Emma sighed heavily. "Anyway, first things first. I've got to figure out how to get some money from the bank so I can buy some new clothes. You're right, I do look a total mess."

CHAPTER 7

Tin Lizzie Gets Cranked

*E*mma had scrubbed her kitchen and returned it to its normal orderly(ish) fashion and was now sitting at her desk busily writing a letter to Mr. Jonathan Doshmore, the manager at her bank.

Dear Mr. Doshmore,

I do hope you and your family are well and I hope to visit you in the very near future.

This letter will be delivered to you by hand by my great niece and also my namesake, Emma Puff. I'm assuming if you are reading this, then you have already met the poor unfortunate child. As I have a cold at the moment, it is not possible for me to come in person.

I instruct you to give my niece the sum of two thousand pounds sterling today, and I also instruct you to make her the sole beneficiary to my will.

You can send the papers to me, for signature, at your convenience. Thank you.

Yours sincerely,

Emma Puff

"I hope this will sort things out, Rusty," Emma said, folding the letter and putting it into an envelope.

"Tomorrow we're going into the city, but right now," she opened the kitchen cupboard and pulled out brooms and buckets, "We're going to check up on Tin Lizzie, my old car, give her a dusting, spruce her up a bit."

"Don't you think you should see if Tin Lizzie will start up first, before you clean her?" I asked as I followed her to the barn.

"Of course not, Rusty." she said, laughing as she pulled at the old barn door that shuddered and creaked, dropping cobwebs and dust all over my head. "First, she has to look good. Then she will feel good. Then who knows what will happen and anyway, she may have just rusted away."

"Nope, she's still here." I said, peeping into the barn as Emma finally managed to push the door wide open.

Sitting in the middle of the barn, covered in thick cobwebs and dust and grit and looking very sorry for herself, was Emma's faithful old car.

"Oh dear," said Emma, pulling handfuls of sticky cobwebs from Tin Lizzie's bonnet, then opening her door and looking inside. "I think a little mouse has been living in here, but it will all clean up."

Mr. Musk perched on the bonnet above the engine and was lifting his claws, now covered with dusty, sticky strands one after the other. He also managed to get the cobwebs all over his bright red beak and blue feathers. "It will all clean up! It will all clean up!" he repeated over and over.

You have to admire their optimism.

"Right, let's get started," said Emma, rolling up her sleeves and grabbing the broom to sweep the cobwebs away.

"What can I do to help?" I asked politely, but I thought to myself, Not a lot.

I was surprised when Emma replied, "You can make use of your paws and scrape off the mess on the back seat. But be careful with the leather."

I set to work. It was quite fun once I got into it.

An hour or so later, Emma and I stood back admiring our handywork.

"Wow!" I exclaimed. The ancient car now shone and sparkled. I could see my reflection in the chrome lights. The leather seats that were worn and covered in dust and mouse droppings, now shone and smelt of polish. "Great job, Emma. She looks so much better and smells nicer too."

I jumped in and put my paws on the driving wheel, "So, do you think she will start?"

Emma was tossing things out of an old wooden trunk that sat in the corner of the barn.

She raised up her arm holding a large funny shaped metal rod. "We need this. It's a crank."

"What's a crank?" I asked.

Emma pushed the end of the crank into a hole in the front of the car. "It's what starts the car," she said. "You put it in the hole and then you turn it like this." She huffed using both hands to wind the rod around. But the car remained silent.

Emma tried several more times at winding the rod, huffing and puffing and stamping her feet in frustration.

"Oh, just start will you, you stupid car!" she yelled on her last attempt, before throwing the crank down and plonking herself down onto the floor, exhausted. She was very sweaty, and the sweat made streaks in the dust as it ran down her cheeks. At first, I thought she might be crying, so I nuzzled her hand. "You were right, Rusty," she puffed. "Lizzie won't start."

I was just about to comfort her with kind words, refraining from saying "I told you so." when she jumped up. "I've got an idea. Wait there, I'll be back in a jiffy!" She ran out of the barn and returned moments later, carrying her old basket that clinked and rattled as she put it down next to Lizzie.

"What are you up to now, Emma?" I asked, watching her lift the car bonnet with one hand whilst holding a tiny bottle in the other and sticking her head inside.

"Well," she said from under the bonnet. "If this magical purple liquid that I made can make us young and make you talk..."

She closed the bonnet and put the crank back into the hole and started to wind. "I think it might make Lizzy start."

"OH WOW!" Emma cried out as Lizzie's engine spluttered into action.

Lizzie whirred, then whizzed, then banged and puffed out smoke from her exhaust pipe. She rattled and chugged and banged again.

"It worked, it worked!" screeched Emma, jumping up and down. "Rusty, can you believe this?"

"Wow." I said. "That stuff definitely has super magical powers."

Mr. Musk returned to the bonnet and seemed to enjoy sitting there being shaken about, because for once he had nothing to say.

Emma opened the door and climbed onto the driver's seat. I watched as she perched onto the very edge of it, trying every angle to reach the pedals with her feet.

I shouted above the engine noise, "You can't drive it, Emma. Your legs aren't long enough to reach the floor."

She sat back on the seat with her arms stretched out to reach the steering wheel. She could only just about touch it with her fingertips. There was no way could she see over the top of the steering wheel.

"You're just not big enough, Emma, and as I have already told you, you are not old enough to drive anymore."

"Oh, *poppycock!*" she yelled, jumping out of the car and slamming the door.

As she stomped out of the barn with a face like thunder and Mr. Musk on her shoulder, she insisted, "I will drive my car, Rusty, but maybe not today. I'll just have to make a few minor adjustments."

Mr. Musk looked straight at me. "Poppycock! Adjustments! Adjustments!"

Oh, how I wish he was an egg.

CHAPTER 8

Let's Go Down to the River

We sat quietly in the kitchen. Emma was munching through an apple then began waving it at me. "I've really missed eating these. It's impossible to eat an apple when you have no good teeth to bite with."

"Is that why you've just eaten three, one after the other?" I asked.

Emma smiled, took another apple from the fruit bowl, and said, "Make that four, Rusty."

She looked at the clock and said, "Let's go down to the river. School's out and maybe those children will be there. You know the ones I used to watch swinging on that tyre."

"You used to tell them off for shouting," I reminded her. You told them to go home and read a book."

Emma laughed, "I know, I was very grumpy sometimes. But now I'm about their age I want to go and meet them and have a go on that tyre swing if they'll let me. It'll be fun."

We followed the path that led to the woods and we could hear laughter. Emma quickened her pace, so I ran in front of her because I wanted to get there first.

"Hey, Rusty!" she squealed. "Wait for me!"

We scrambled up to the top of the hill, both out of breath. There, below us, sitting under the big oak tree, were four giggling children.

Emma sat down on the old tree trunk, where she'd sat many times before when she was old. She'd spent hours sitting and watching the children play, and sometimes (when she was in a good mood) she'd brought them homemade biscuits.

A boy with tight curly black hair, brown skin, and the biggest brown eyes I've ever seen turned and pointed up to us, then after saying something to the other three, they all ran up the hill towards us.

"Hey," they shouted in unison, with big smiles.

"Oh, what a cute puppy," said a girl dressed all in pink, with brown curly hair and lots of freckles on her turned up nose. She scooped me up and stroked me gently.

"His name is Rusty," said Emma.

"We haven't seen you before. Have you just moved here?" asked the boy with the big brown eyes. He was wearing blue jeans and a red t-shirt that had what looked like his dinner all down the front of it.

"Yes, I'm staying with my great aunt." replied Emma.

"Wow," exclaimed the boy. "You mean great, like huge, big, or fat or something?"

"Leroy, you are such a blockhead!" said the tallest boy with glasses that peeked out from under his black baseball cap. He was also wearing blue jeans and a black t-shirt with a lot of writing on it. "Great aunt means she is the sister to one of your grandparents."

Leroy shrugged his shoulders, "All right, Mr. Know-It-All, but stop calling me blockhead, okay?"

He turned to Emma. "I'm Leroy," he pointed to the girl, "and her name is Sacha." He nodded his head towards the other two boys.

"The one wearing the glasses, Mr. Know-It-All, is Tom, but we call him Specs."

"And I'm Spike." interrupted the other boy, taking off his baseball cap and bowing to Emma.

His blue jeans were ripped and muddy. His hair was long and blonde. He pointed to his jeans and said with a big smile, "Yeah, I fell out of the tree!"

"My name is Emma, and I'd love to have a go on that," she said pointing to a huge tyre hanging over the water from a rope that was tied to a branch of the towering oak tree.

"Whoop, whoop! C'mon then." They squealed as they raced back down the hill.

It was at the very moment when they reached the tree that all four of them stopped and stared at Emma's clothes. The newspaper was hanging out of her shoes and the pink wool that she had used as a belt to keep her make-do skirt up was trailing down her legs.

Emma's face blushed a tomato red as she suddenly remembered how she looked. "Oh, erm, err, yes, sorry." She stammered as she tried to hide the pink wool. "I, err, I lost my bag on the train and, err, erm," she mumbled as she stuffed the paper back into her shoes "my aunt is taking me to the city tomorrow to get new clothes."

"What a bummer," exclaimed Spike. "I lost my school bag on the train once. It had all my homework in it," he said sitting down next to Emma and passing her some bits of newspaper. "I got into so much trouble from Ferret Face, my form master."

Sacha butted in, "Oh, you are sooo lucky, Emma. New clothes! I love shopping for new clothes. I wish I could lose my clothes! I'm going to the city tomorrow. I could meet you and help you choose if you like?"

Emma's eyes widened. "Oh, yes, please, Sacha, thank you!" she replied, before tossing her shoes aside, hoisting up her skirt and climbing onto the giant tyre. Specs grinned, taking hold of the rope. "How high do you want to go?" he asked, as he started to swing the tyre. "All the way up, please!" said Emma. "As high as I can go!"

I covered my eyes with my paws.

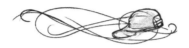

CHAPTER 9

I Dare You

Leroy stood shivering in just his underpants with his coat around his shoulders. His blue jeans and red t-shirt were draped over a branch of the tree along with his chunky trainers, dripping with water.

Everyone had been swinging on the tyre and daring each other to do stupid things.

It started with Sasha daring Emma to hold on with one hand and ended with Spike daring Leroy to swing upside down holding onto the tyre with the back of his knees.

"That's not fair!" Leroy said when Spike announced his dare to him.

"Revenge for putting salt on my trifle," laughed Spike.

Leroy managed to stay on the tyre for about a minute, then fell headfirst into the water to an uproar of laughter and cheering.

"Oh jeez, my mum's gonna kill me!" Leroy cried out as he stood knee deep in the water, watching his new red baseball cap drift away. Then, looking at Spike, he shouted "It's all your fault. My mum only just got that hat for me!"

"Hey, calm down buddy," said Spike, putting his arm across Leroy's shoulders. "I'll get you another one."

Spike smiled earnestly at Leroy. "Look, you can go home with my hat and tell your mum that we've swapped for a couple of days. She'll be fine about it!"

"That's a fantastic idea," said Sasha. "Emma and I are going shopping tomorrow, so we can buy a new one for you!"

"What am I going to say about my clothes being soaking wet? And I'm freezing!" grumbled Leroy as he jumped up and down trying to keep himself warm. "My mum is gonna go ape!"

"Come back to my house." suggested Spike. "My mum can dry your stuff in her dryer. She won't mind. You can stay for dinner, and your mum will never know."

As I watched and listened to these children, I began to understand what true friendship means. Us dogs don't think twice about stealing each other's bones and toys, let alone getting one another in trouble.

We all began to walk up the hill when Sasha asked "Do any of you remember that old lady? I think her name was also Emma. She used to sit up there on the log and watch us."

"Yeah, I do." said Specs "Sometimes she gave us biscuits. They were so good."

"And she had an old dog!" added Spike.

Leroy, who was jumping rather than walking, pointed his finger at Emma and said, "Come to think of it, I'm pretty sure her dog was also called Rusty!"

Emma looked at the four inquisitive faces, "That's my aunt! I'm named after her, so I thought I'd call my puppy the same as her dog."

"Oh, that's real cool," shivered Leroy. "But your aunt, she is so old!"

"Sometimes she would be nice to us," said Spike. "She'd chat to us and give us homemade biscuits and other times she was, well, really grumpy and told us to be quiet or to go home and read a book."

"Is she the old lady that helps all the animals, you know, makes medicines and stuff?" asked Sacha.

"And lives in that old stone cottage in the woods?" asked Specs. "That place looks real creepy to me, looks like it has ghosts and stuff!"

"Yes, that's her," replied Emma.

"And yes, she can be grumpy." She giggled. "But not so much nowadays." She stopped at the path that led to her cottage and asked. "Why don't you all come for tea tomorrow afternoon about five and I'll introduce you to Mr. Musk?" She looked over to Specs, "He's not a ghost. He's my aunt's parrot, and he loves visitors."

After a unanimous "Yes, please!" we made our way home.

CHAPTER 10

Buses, Banks, and Bold Emma

I was in a deep sleep and slowly waking up to the wonderful smell of bread baking.

I opened one eye and could see Emma. She was busily filling the fridge with all sorts of delicious food. It was still dark. She must've been up half the night.

"Good morning, Emma. What are you doing?" I asked while stretching my back legs and having a good old shake.

"Morning, Rusty. We have a busy morning, first the bank, then shopping." she said, dipping her finger into a bowl of chocolate fudge and licking it. "Then back here for tea."

"What are you going to say to your new friends, Emma?" I asked.

"About what? What am I going to say to my friends about what, Rusty?" she replied, taking the bread from the oven.

"What are you going to say about where your 'great aunt' is, Emma? You know, the old lady you. The one that is missing. The one that is not ninety years old anymore. The one that is now a child with a ninety-year-old's brain."

"Oh, that." she said, seemingly without a care. "I don't know right now, but something will come to me, I'm sure."

She picked me up and plonked me in her basket. "You can go in here. We've got a bus to catch.

I loved the bus ride. Seeing things fly past so quickly was so exciting! The last time I travelled fast was years ago when Emma was driving her car, but I'd kept my eyes closed for most of that.

The city was very noisy and smelt of fumes. I walked on a leash closely beside Emma.

I had to keep dodging what looked like a sea of different types of shoes and boots, hundreds of them, and I didn't like it.

Everyone was stopping and staring at Emma as she walked towards the bank.

Today's outfit was a pair of bright orange pants that she cut the bottoms off in an effort to make them fit her. She once again tied the pink wool around her waist to keep them up. But the crotch was down past her knees and where she cut the bottoms off the legs, they were fraying with every step she took. The orange cottons were getting caught on the newspaper that was now beginning to pop out of her shoes.

We entered the bank, a grand building, with high ceilings and marble floors. It smelt of furniture polish. Men in suits, carrying briefcases, were either rushing across the marble floor with expressionless faces or reading newspapers.

A few women stood behind a long, carved piece of polished wood, wearing nice clothes. They wore some sort of face paint. I mostly noticed a red color on their lips. They started whispering to each other and stared at Emma with surprise and amusement as she walked towards the banker's desk.

The newspaper was now trailing out of her worn-out shoes, with long strands of orange cotton matted onto it from her fraying trousers legs. I could tell by the way she was walking, or should I say hobbling, that the shoes had definitely lost their grip on her feet.

The bright pink wool that was holding up the ridiculously bright orange pants had come loose and was now trailing down the back of her legs, getting caught on the paper and orange cottons.

Emma pulled the envelope out of her basket and waved it for the banker to see. "Excuse me. Hello, can you see me?"

"Good morning, young lady. How can I help? Have you lost your parents?" the banker smiled, looking down at Emma.

"No, I have not lost my parents," retorted Emma.

"No, but you've nearly lost your pants!" I added. I was really starting to enjoy this talking thing.

Emma glared daggers at me, then looked back up at the man who was staring down at her and continued in her most important sounding voice. "My name is Emma Puff, great-niece of Emma Puff, who has banked with this bank for seventy years." Then, holding the letter high and waving it further towards him, she said, "This is for Mr. Doshmore to read immediately, please!"

CHAPTER 11

Money, Please

$\mathcal{M}$r. Doshmore was sitting on a large brown leather chair behind his huge desk in his plush office.

He held Emma's letter in his right hand, removed his large horn-rimmed glasses and stared directly at Emma and me.

I was on Emma's lap, and she was fidgeting nervously as she sat on the chair opposite him. Finally, he said, "I'm sorry to read that your aunt is not well, Emma. I've known her since I became the manager of the bank, come to think of it," he said with a smile. "I owe her a visit."

"I'm sure she'd appreciate a visit from you, Mr. Doshmore. She speaks fondly of you." said Emma sweetly. "When can I tell her you will be coming?"

"You can tell her I will bring the papers she asked for tomorrow," he said.

Then he stood up, "Excuse me a minute," and left his office.

Oh boy, I thought to myself, this was getting more and more complicated. How long can Emma pretend she is her own niece?

Mr. Doshmore reappeared and handed Emma a large brown envelope. "Now this is a lot of money that your aunt has instructed me to give to you, so be sure to be very careful with it. Keep it hidden and, for goodness sake, please don't lose it!"

Emma thanked Mr. Doshmore and stuffed the large envelope containing the money deep into her basket.

At last! We left the bank, and I was very grateful that Emma let me stop next to a lamp post. I was just about to speak,\ when Emma's orange pants fell down around her ankles, revealing a huge pair of white bloomers, also secured with the pink wool, that started flapping in the wind.

"EEK!" cried Emma, as she desperately tried to pull them up, tripping over the pink wool that was tangled everywhere.

"Help me, Rusty!" she cried as she was getting more and more tangled up with wool.

"Yes, Emma, don't worry," I said as I tried pulling the wool away from her shoes with my teeth.

"No, Rusty, not that bit, or my bloomers will come down," she yelled. She toppled over and landed next to me with the orange pants on her head just as a lorry drove past, spraying a puddle all over us.

"It's OK. It's OK," said Sasha, covering Emma with her pink coat. "Looks like I arrived just in time," she said laughing and helping Emma up. "Sorry for laughing, but you did look funny."

"It's so embarrassing. All those people just stared at me. You saved me, Sasha," mumbled Emma, holding the coat tightly and looking at the pavement. "Thank you."

Sasha took my leash and asked, "Where's your aunt?"

"She didn't feel well, so she stayed at home," replied Emma. "But I've got lots of money, so we can still go shopping!"

Sasha smiled and grabbed Emma's hand. "The sooner, the better, Emma," she said, trying not to laugh.

CHAPTER 12

Burgers and Bright Pink Wool

I sat in Emma's basket on the floor of the changing room. So many clothes were getting heaped beside me. Jeans, t-shirts, sweaters, coats, dresses, panties, socks, nightdresses, and pairs of trainers, shoes, and boots. I was afraid I'd get buried alive.

The two friends umm-ed, aah-ed and giggled whilst parading up and down in front of the mirrors, trying on everything, saying, "Oh, that colour is good on you!" or "Do these look too big on me?" or "Does my *bum* look big in this?" and then bursting into laughter. This went on for what felt like hours.

I have decided that shopping, the city, and banks are not for me.

Sasha gathered up armfuls of garments and passed them to the assistant, asking her to wrap them. She also pointed out what Emma arrived in and asked her to throw it away since Emma would be wearing a new outfit immediately.

"Wow, Emma, you look great," said Sasha as Emma stepped out from the dressing room, wearing her new blue jeans, red t-shirt, and the latest trendy red *trainers*.

Emma did a twirl, picked up her new blue coat, and with the happiest face she said, "Thank you so much, Sasha, I couldn't have chosen all these without your help."

"I've loved every moment, my pleasure," replied Sasha. "But there's one more thing," she said, picking up Emma's basket and holding it up high, "this, my friend, has got to go."

Both girls burst out laughing.

I was not amused. I'd lost my ride!

"I've just remembered, we have to get Leroy a new hat," said Emma.

"Yes, we do. But we have to go to the sports shop to get the same one, and guess what?" Sasha grinned. "It's right next door to the Burger Bar, and I'm starving."

To my horror, Emma lifted me up and placed me into her new backpack. "Hey, what are you doing?" I asked as I tried to escape.

"This is perfect for you, Rusty. You will love it," she said.

Surprisingly, I fitted nicely, with enough room for my head to stick up out of the top. Then with Sasha's help, she put the backpack on her back.

Once I had gotten used to being bounced up and down as Emma walked, it wasn't too bad, apart from Emma's long hair tickling my nose. At least I didn't have to dodge shoes and boots!

Oh, give me burgers every day of my life. They are yummy. Although, I didn't care much for the place where we were eating them. It was a big restaurant, filled to the brim with young people, eating and laughing together. Also, a few families, some with crying babies. The noise was deafening.

"These are so (hic) good," mumbled Emma, as she tried to stifle her hiccups. "I love the (hic) sauce and the (hic) cheese."

"You shouldn't talk with food in your mouth," I hissed.

"Slow down. You look like you've never eaten a burger before," laughed Sasha. With a look of astonishment, she watched as Emma sucked and sucked the straw

protruding from a large paper cup, until it made a loud gurgling sound. Emma then let out the biggest burp Sasha had ever heard.

"Emma!" exclaimed Sasha, as she looked behind her, hoping that the boys sitting there had not heard.

"Tell me the truth, you've never had a burger and a large fizzy pop before, have you?"

Emma looked at her friend, shook her head, and said, "I was never allowed to have a burger or drink fizzy pop. My grandfather, who used to look after me, was very strict. He would say anything that wasn't a vegetable was the devil's food and it would send you mad. That included cakes and sweets, but my aunt lets me eat everything."

Sasha asked, "What happened to your parents?"

"They died a long time ago," said Emma.

"Wow, you've just said something true, Emma," I remarked.

"Oh, that's sad," said Sasha. "So, what happened to your grandfather for him to send you to your great aunt?"

"Nothing happened to him," said Emma meekly. "He just announced he was sending me to Aunt Emma. He put my things in a bag and Rusty in my arms and put me on the train, and here I am," she smiled.

"Weird thing to do," said a puzzled Sasha. Then, glancing at her watch, she said. "Come on, let's pick up all the shopping bags and get going. We have to catch the bus."

How Emma thinks up such nonsense is beyond me. I know there is absolutely no way she can ever tell the whole truth. Whatever will come out of her mouth next?

The bus ride home was horrible. There was constant chatter about everyone coming to Emma's for tea, and I was squashed between all the shopping.

Emma said goodbye to Sasha and said they would see each other at five o'clock for tea. Then, after dropping all her shopping onto the hall floor, she opened the kitchen door. "Fiddlesticks!" she cried, as she took in the sight before her.

Mr. Musk was sitting on the edge of the table, with bright pink wool hanging from his beak, scraps of newspaper stuck in his feathers and long strands of pink yarn tangled around his claws! He dipped his head and looked at Emma. "I've got nothing to wear, Emma! Nothing to wear! Nothing! Nothing!"

"What have you done? You naughty parrot! Oh, what a mess!" she said, looking around the kitchen in despair.

Bright pink wool was stretched and tangled from the light to the cupboards, from the cupboards to the clock on the wall, from the clock on the wall to the range, from the range to the kitchen table, the chairs, and the sink taps.

Little scraps of orange fabric were draped here and there over the wool, and the kitchen sink was full of pieces of newspaper.

It looked like a giant pink spider's web had completely taken over the kitchen.

"Oh a mess! Oh a mess! What have you done!" squawked the parrot, looking at Rusty.

Emma should have tidied up this morning. I've noticed, now that she is young, she is very messy.

I saw this chaos as the perfect opportunity to finally convince Emma to put Mr. Musk behind bars. "He needs to go in his cage when you go out, Emma. He always makes some sort of mess."

She glared at me. "You, Rusty, were much more fun when you couldn't talk."

CHAPTER 13

Meet Mr. Musk

*E*verything was spic and span again, and Emma was now busy making sandwiches.

Mr. Musk was sitting quietly on the curtain pole, preening his blue feathers. It had taken Emma ages to cut the cottons from his claws. Stupid parrot.

"They will be here soon, it's nearly five o'clock. What are you going to say to them about 'Aunt Emma?'" I asked, looking up at her.

"That she's not well and is staying in bed, or shall I just tell them the truth, Rusty?" she said sarcastically, throwing her apron on the chair.

"I know you can't do that, Emma. I'm just a little worried how this will all end up, that's all." "Well, please don't worry, Rusty. Think of it as a big adventure, loosen up, and have some fun!"

I scrambled from my basket, my tail wagging like crazy, I could hear voices and laughter coming up the garden path. The old cottage was suddenly full of chatter and laughter.

Emma's friends had never seen such a collection of ancient objects and believe me, there were plenty.

"What's this?" asked Spike, waving what resembled a tennis racket made of steel.

"It's a carpet beater," replied Emma. "Years ago, before electricity and vacuum cleaners, people would throw their rugs over the washing line and beat them to remove the dust and dirt."

"And this?" enquired Leroy, holding the handle of a rectangle board with grooves along it. He was strumming it with his fingers, as if it were a guitar.

"I don't think you will get much of a tune from that," said Emma, laughing, as she placed the new red baseball cap on his head.

"Wow, you remembered," said Leroy. "It's the same. It's great, thanks."

Emma pointed to Leroy's 'guitar.' "This is a scrubbing board. People used it to clean their clothes. They would get them all soapy and rub them up and down on the grooves to get the dirt off."

"This place is crazy. It's like a museum," added Specs, as he stared up at the tall grandfather clock.

"You lot are so rude. Stop touching everything," blurted Sasha, standing with her hands on her hips. "You should wait until Emma's aunt is in the room and ask her permission before pulling the place apart!"

Sasha looked at Emma. "Talking of your aunt, where is she?"

Before Emma could answer, Mr. Musk flew down from the curtain pole, perched on top of the grandfather clock, shook his blue feathers, dipped his yellow head and squawked,

"This place is crazy! Pull the place apart! Where is she! Where is she! You lot are so rude!"

Sasha let out a huge "EEK!" and dove under the table.

"He won't hurt you Sasha, he's only a parrot, " said Emma. "He just repeats everything he hears."

The three boys looked at the parrot in amazement. They all grinned the same devilish grin as they glanced at each other, then back at Mr. Musk.

I knew exactly what they were thinking.

"I'm OK. Sorry, he gave me a fright, made me jump," explained Sasha, crawling out from under the table.

"You are such a wimp sometimes Sasha," said Specs. "Fancy being scared of a parrot."

"Yeah, that's so lame." chirped in Spike and Leroy.

"I'm not scared of him." retorted Sasha. "He made me jump."

"Well, prove it then," said Specs. "Go and talk to him."

Sasha stood up and marched over to the grandfather clock, where Mr. Musk was still perched. She looked up at him, and said in a very loud voice,

"Boys are stupid. Boys are dumb. Leroy, Specs, and Spike all have a big bum."

Mr. Musk stared down at Sasha, cocked his head to the left and then to the right, put his claw into his red beak and nibbled on it, then rustled his blue feathers, stood tall, and merrily squawked, "Boys are stupid! Boys are dumb! Leroy, Specs, and Spike all have a big bum!"

All five children collapsed onto the floor in uncontrollable laughter.

Mr. Musk flew into the living room and the boys followed whispering things to each other, "He repeats whatever you say!" and "Oh boy, this could be fun!"

The girls stayed behind. "So where is your aunt, Emma? Surely, she must be wondering what's going on with all this noise?" asked Sasha, as she tickled my tummy. I loved it.

"She can't hear you. She has taken out her hearing aid and is staying in bed as she's still not feeling too well."

"Oh, poor thing, do you think she will be all right?"

"She will be fine. She is reading her book, eating chocolate, and cuddling her dog."

Now Emma is telling fancy lies. Hearing aid! Chocolate! Cuddling her dog! How does she think this stuff up? I was never allowed into her bedroom, let alone on her bed.

"It sounds like the boys are having fun with Mr. Musk," said Emma, hearing shrieks of laughter coming from the living room.

Sasha frowned, and shaking her head, she mumbled, "Three boys alone with a talking parrot is a recipe for disaster."

"Okay," said Emma "Let's set the table for tea and get the boys away from Mr. Musk.

I'm starving again, and there's lots of delicious treats in the fridge."

CHAPTER 14

So Much Fun, So Much Mess

The tea table looked like it was set for a king. All sorts of sandwiches, little sausages on sticks, chocolate fudge cake, trifle, iced cupcakes, banana muffins, shortbread, and a bottle of every flavour of fizzy soda pop.

"Wow," said Leroy. "No wonder your aunt needed to lie down after making all this."

"I think I might need to lie down after eating it." laughed Spike. "And look at that yummy trifle. It's got my name written all over it."

"Don't any of you dare sit down at the table until you've washed your hands," insisted Sasha as she stood next to the sink, pointing at the soap and holding up a towel.

"All right, little Miss Bossy Boots," Specs said, turning on the tap, and flicking water at her face.

Sasha flicked his ear with the towel. "You've probably got millions of germs on your hands, so wash 'em."

Emma closed the living room door. "I think Mr. Musk should stay in there while we have tea, or he may get too excited."

"What you really mean, Emma, is 'Or you might feel sick when he poops,'" I said.

Oh, if looks could kill.

For the first time since the children had arrived, they were quiet, apart from the occasional "Oh, this is yummy." or "What's in this?" and "Can I have more, please?"

But it didn't last long.

I can honestly say (because I was watching) that what followed did start as an accident...

Spike was tucking in to his second bowl of trifle when Sasha nudged him. This caused him to drop his spoon, full of trifle, which landed on the edge of his plate, with the handle of the spoon pointing towards Leroy. Leroy hastily jumped up to help his friend, slipped and his hand came down hard on to the spoon handle, sending the trifle hurtling across the table to land on Specs's specs.

Specs was just about to put a spoonful of chocolate fudge cake into his mouth when the trifle landed. He immediately responded by flicking his spoon toward Spike. He missed, and it landed on Sasha's pink shirt.

Sasha was about to take a bite out of her sticky iced cupcake but retaliated instantly and hurled it towards Specs, but it landed on Emma's head.

Emma burst into uncontrollable giggles, scooped up a handful of trifle, and threw it at Leroy's nose. A direct hit. Leroy was about to drink his soda but chucked it over Spike's head.

Then it was absolute chaos, food flying everywhere, with shrieks of "Take that then," "No, not in my hair." "Oh, you dollop." "Ha ha, got yah." "Yes! On target." And, "Ouch!" as cake, trifle, half-eaten sandwiches, and fizzy pop hurtled in every direction across the table.

All five sat back on their chairs, exhausted from laughing, with big grins on their faces together with jam, cream, chocolate fudge, soggy lettuce, bits of tomato, and trifle. Their hair was matted with jelly and cream, and their clothes were covered in chocolate fudge and soda. The floor was a soggy mess with bits of cake, and half-eaten sandwiches floating in a sea of brown liquid. Even the walls were dripping with goo.

Emma giggled as she wiped a lump of jelly from her forehead. "That was the best fun I've ever had. It was sooo funny!"

"My tummy hurts 'cause I laughed so much," said Leroy, holding his arms across his bulging stomach.

"Mine too," giggled Specs.

"And the look on your face, Sasha," laughed Spike, "when that muffin hit you on the nose and stayed there, you went cross-eyed!"

"Yeah, I did," giggled Sasha. "It was the best fun ever." Then, pointing to the awful mess, she asked, "But what do we do now? And look at our clothes. My mum's gonna go ape."

"Yeah, mine too," chorused the three boys.

"What's your aunt gonna say, Emma, when she sees this?" asked Leroy.

Emma opened the cupboard, pulled out a mop, bucket, broom, scrubbing brush, and a pile of cleaning cloths. Then, passing them to the boys, she said, "She's not going to see or say anything. Come on, let's clean up."

Everyone was busy, sweeping, washing, and scrubbing, when Emma said,

"Tell your *mums* the truth. Please don't lie to them. Just tell them we had a food fight, and it was the best fun ever. They were kids once you know, and if you tell them all about it, they will probably laugh with you. After all, deep down, I have a feeling that every kid, no matter how old they are, would have loved it. And you and your clothes will wash clean, so no harm done."

CHAPTER 15

Mr. Doshmore Gets a Shock

*E*mma woke up late this morning and was rushing around mumbling to herself about the impending visit from Mr. Doshmore, the bank manager. He was coming to visit her "aunt" about some papers she had to sign.

At least the kitchen was restored to normal, apart from chocolate stains on the wall.

The grandfather clock wasn't looking too good.

Mr. Musk spent most of his time yesterday afternoon perched on it. Emma frantically tried to wash the awful mess, She also forgot to take the blanket off the bird's cage and set him free. The peace and quiet were bliss.

"Emma, could I have my breakfast, please?" I asked. "I know you're busy, but my tummy's rumbling."

"Oh, gosh, sorry, Rusty," she sighed, pouring some food into my bowl, "I'm just trying to sort out the clock. Oh, and poor Mr. Musk, I've forgotten him too," she huffed as she uncovered his cage and opened his door, pouring seeds into his dish.

I pricked up my ears. "A car just stopped at our gate, Emma."

"Doshmore's here. Oh, lumpy cold gravy!" blurted Emma, rushing to the sink and emptying the bucket of disgusting poop water into it. She washed her hands, smoothed down her hair, and cleared her throat. Then she calmly walked to the door and opened it wide, "Good morning, Mr. Doshmore. Please come in."

Mr. Doshmore was a very tall man and had to dip his head to enter the cottage. Standing up straight he said to Emma, "Hello, young lady, how are you today?"

"I'm fine, thank you. Please sit down. Would you like coffee or tea?" she replied.

"Coffee would be nice, thank you," he said as he removed his coat and sat down at the kitchen table.

Emma put the coffee pot onto the range, then said sweetly, "I'm afraid Aunt Emma is still feeling unwell and thinks she might have the flu. She has suggested that I take the papers up to her for her to sign, as she fears if she comes down to see you, you might catch it, as it is very contagious!"

I was actually beginning to believe Emma's stories. She was ever so good.

Emma poured Mr. Doshmore his coffee and placed it in front of him.

"Thank you, Emma. Have you called the doctor?" he asked, as he spooned sugar into his cup.

"I did offer, but she said no need. She said she has had the flu many times in her long life, and the medicine that she has made herself is the best."

"Very well then," he said, opening his large brown briefcase. He passed some papers to Emma. "Tell her to read through everything and if she's happy, to sign where I have penciled a cross."

"Righty ho!" Emma said and ran upstairs.

Mr. Doshmore sat quietly sipping his coffee whilst waiting for Emma's return, when Mr. Musk flew down from the curtain pole and settled on the corner of the kitchen table next to him.

"Hello, Mr. Musk," he said, wiggling his finger at the bird.

Mr. Musk shook his feathers, dipped his head, and slowly walked along the table towards Mr. Doshmore, keeping his beady eyes on the wiggling finger, then he dipped his head left and squawked, "Hi, big dummy! What you saying? Have you pooped ya pants?"

Then, running along the table, "You got big bogeys on ya nose! Ha Ha!" and back again, "Grumpy bear face with dinosaur breath! Ha Ha!"

Then, stopping directly in front of him, "Drop ya pants and shake ya booty! Wahoo! You're a silly bogey from a big snotty nose! Ha Ha Ha!"

Mr. Doshmore spurted out his mouthful of coffee. It went all over his shirt, tie, trousers and shiny shoes. He jumped up, his eyes watering big tear drops and his large horn-rimmed glasses steaming up! He was coughing and spluttering, he couldn't see where he was going, then he tripped over my basket and crashed headfirst against the door.

Mr. Musk flew silently back to his curtain pole, just as Emma returned with the papers. "Oh dear, are you alright?" she asked, thumping Mr. Doshmore on his back. "It sounds like your coffee went down the wrong way!"

Mr. Doshmore flopped back down on his chair. He couldn't speak, he was still coughing, he wiped his runny eyes, and he pointed his finger up to Mr. Musk.

Emma took no notice and passed the papers to him. "She's signed everything and says 'thank you for coming,' and when she has recovered, she will invite you to tea."

Then she helped him with his coat, passed him his briefcase, opened the door, and smiled sweetly. "Get yourself some cough sweets, Mr. Doshmore. There's a shop in the village. Bye!"

As we watched him go down the path, I said, "Emma, it was Mr. Musk. He said some really bad things to Doshmore."

"What things?" she asked, watching him as he coughed his way through the rickety old gate.

At that very same moment, we saw George Cracknall parking his bike.

"Oh, no!" gasped Emma. "Don't say a word, Rusty. Remember, he must not know anything. Not yet, anyway."

"But he can't hear me, Emma," I said.

"Morning, young Emma," huffed George as he walked up the path. "I see you had visitors already this morning..."

"Yes," replied Emma. "Aunt Emma's bank manager. He needed her to sign some papers."

George pulled off his boots and stepped into the kitchen. After a quick look around, taking in that it was all in order, he asked, "Where is she, then?"

"She thinks she has the flu and is staying in bed, as it may be contagious. She signed all the papers for Mr. Doshmore, then said she would have a little sleep. But she's a lot better," insisted Emma.

George sat down at the kitchen table, looked at Emma and said, "So, if your aunt is unwell, how are you looking after yerself? Are you eating?"

"Oh yes, I can cook. I've been making soups and baking cakes."

"And where's Rusty, the old one? He was always the first to greet me when I popped in."

"He's with Aunt Emma, sleeping on her bed."

"What?" exclaimed George, scratching his head. "She would never let that old dog into her bedroom."

"Err, um," stammered Emma "I know, she told me, but old Rusty doesn't like young Rusty. Erm, so she decided to keep him with her until she's better, then she's going to make sure they become friends."

George sighed, rubbing his chin and studying Emma's face. "Hmmm, I see.

So, has your aunt arranged for you to go to school?"

"No, not yet, but she said she would arrange for me to start school after the Christmas holidays. I've already met some children who go there. They're very nice. Aunt Emma said she's glad I'm here to look after her, and she thinks she will be up and about in a couple of days. I'm making sure she eats all her soup and takes her medicine."

George let out another long sigh and another, "Hmmm, I see." I could tell by looking at Emma that she was getting a little nervous.

I decided to help out, so I jumped up at George, wagging my tail, and gave him that look, the one that says, 'play with me!'

It worked. He gave me one of the treats he always carried in his pocket for 'old Rusty.'

Ha! It was meant for me anyway, right? But, of course, he didn't know that.

"How are your knees, Mr. Cracknall?" Emma asked. "You said you were seeing the doctor."

"Still hurting. He gave me some tablets. Taste horrible they do," he said as he wiped his nose again with the large grubby handkerchief. "Anyways, young lady, call me George. I don't like all this 'Mr.' malarkey. I'm just known as George, always have been," he said with a smile, showing that he had very few teeth.

Mr. Musk settled on the edge of the table next to George.

"Morning, Mr. Musk." said George.

"Drop ya pants and shake ya tablets! Wahoo! What you saying? Big snotty nose! Ha, Ha, Ha!"

"Good grief," muttered George.

Emma just sat with her mouth open in disbelief.

"Boogers taste horrible, they do! Mr. Malarkey! Ha Ha!" continued the idiotic bird, as he bobbed his head up and down, running along the table.

"MR. MUSK!" shrieked Emma, banging her hand on the table in an effort to shut the bird up. Then Emma burst out into a huge belly laugh. Laughing uncontrollably, she fell off her chair. "Did the boys teach you talk like that?!"

CHAPTER 16

Big Driving Shoes

I lay in my favourite spot in the garden enjoying the sunshine. I was just about to doze off when suddenly a welly boot landed on my head. Clanking and thumping noises were coming from the garden shed and I could hear Emma shouting, "Where's my glue?" so I decide to go and investigate.

Every old welly boot that she had ever owned lay scattered over the yard, together with an ancient mattress that had loads of curly springs sticking out of it.

A sweaty, dusty Emma, carrying garden shears and her tin of glue, a tape measure draped around her neck, stumbled out into the sunlight.

I gave her a curious look and asked, "Whatever are you up to now?" as she collected the boots and put them in a pile.

"I have an idea, Rusty." she said, with that determined look on her face as she measured her new *trainers*. "I'm going to make some big shoes, some very big shoes, so I can drive my car!"

"Really? With that pile of junk, Emma? Now I know for sure you're still completely bonkers," I said, trying to laugh, but my lips wouldn't curl up, so I looked like I was growling. "Well, this I've got to see." So

I settled down to be entertained while Emma began cutting the big rubber soles off the *welly boots.*

I must have dozed off after boot number eight met its fate with the garden shears.

I was having a lovely dream with a big juicy bone when I heard Mr. Musk gibbering, "Err, yuk! This glue! Sticky mess! Sticky mess!"

I opened my eyes, and in front of my nose were two huge towers of thick rubber soles, all stuck together. They went up and up. I couldn't see the top. I stood up, but they were taller than me and as I looked up, I saw each tower of rubber soles had been crowned with one of Emma's new *trainers.* Mr. Musk was perched on top of the left one. "Oh screaming hedge hogs! This glue, wah!" he jabbered over and over.

Emma was on her knees with the carving knife in her hand, slicing her way through the old mattress.

I told her "No way can you walk in those ridiculous shoes, Emma. You will fall over and break your neck."

"I don't intend to walk in them, Rusty. They are my driving shoes." Then, lifting up a square piece of the mattress and looking at it, she asked, "Does this look about the size of the car seat?"

"Yes possibly," I replied, absolutely dreading what she was going to say next.

She stood up and put the mattress square under her arm, then carefully picked up a giant shoe by its laces in each hand. She had to hold her arms up high because the ridiculous shoes were so tall. Mr. Musk, thinking he had been invited, immediately perched on her right arm. Looking down at me, she said "Well, come on then. Let's go and find out."

Emma carefully placed the ridiculous shoes next to the driver's door. Upon seeing that the mattress square fitted perfectly on the driving seat, she gave herself a pat on the back.

"Just look at that, Rusty. Made to measure! I'm so proud of myself," she said, beaming a satisfied smile at me. "I'll be able to see where I'm going."

"Yeah, probably straight into a bush," I muttered.

"Now I need to see if these shoes are going to be long enough," she said, climbing into the car. Then, with her feet dangling mid-air out of the door, she grabbed the silly shoes, put her feet in, and tied up the laces.

"Emma, are you serious?" I laughed. "You look like you should be in a circus with the clowns."

The shoes were nearly longer than her legs.

She slowly eased herself back on the seat and swung her legs into the car.

"Yes!" she yelled. "Yes, I can reach the pedals. I can reach the steering wheel and I can see through the window screen. Whoop, whoop. This is fantastic!" she cried, bouncing up and down.

Mr. Musk was observing from the bonnet of the car, perched right on top of the hood ornament trying to look important. He had such a high opinion of himself.

He bopped up and down ruffling his feathers squawking over and over, "Fantastic whoop! I can see! I can reach!"

I looked up at Emma's beaming face, so full of pride and excitement, and I knew nothing was going to stop her. I asked, "When are you going to take Tin Lizzie out for a drive?"

CHAPTER 17

Stop the Car!

*E*mma sat at the kitchen table carefully removing the lens from her old glasses. She popped them on her nose "Look," she said, "remind you of anyone?" Then she tied up her long hair and placed her bonkers red feathered hat on her head. "There, perfect," she said looking into the mirror. "If anyone sees me driving, they will just think it's the old Emma Puff."

I said a silent prayer and felt butterflies in my tummy as I followed her out of the kitchen to the barn.

Emma's crank started Lizzie, and the ancient car immediately whirred into action, spluttering and puffing out smoke from her rear. I reluctantly climbed onto the passenger seat, followed by Mr. Musk, who perched on the dashboard. Tin Lizzie was shaking and rattling as we waited for Emma to put on her driving shoes.

"Oh, don't look so nervous, Rusty. This will be fun." she said, as the car shot forward out of the barn.

"I don't believe that for one moment!" I shrieked, as we bounced down the drive with loud bangs coming from Lizzie's tailpipe.

"Oh, this is fantastic. Driving again!" laughed Emma, as we turned onto the lane.

"Emma!" I yelled. "You should have stopped to see if anything was coming!"

"Oh, Rusty. Don't worry about little things like that," Emma said.

I closed my eyes and said another prayer.

Mr. Musk bounced up and down and slid back and forth on the dashboard as the car shot forward in spurts, then slowed again. When Emma looked to the left, the car swerved right and vice versa.

"Emma, keep your eyes on the road and drive straight." I instructed, trying not to slip off my seat. "Stop looking everywhere, and tell me, where are we supposed to be going?"

"Relax, Rusty." She said, brushing the feathers away from her face that were flopping down from her hat, causing the car to swerve up onto the grass bank and bump down again. "Emma!" I screeched as I slid onto the floor.

"Oops. Sorry," she giggled.

Mr. Musk was squawking, "Oops. Sorry, Emma! Oops. Sorry, Emma!" as he slid gracefully up and down the dashboard.

As we came around a bend, Emma gasped. "That looks like George on his bike up ahead!"

I peered through the window. "You're right, Emma. It's him."

"Oh, no. I can't drive past him. He mustn't see us!" she cried out as the car swerved and shook.

I nodded to the right and said, "Look over there. It's a dirt road. Drive down it quickly, Emma, or he might turn around and see us."

"Yes, yes, I see it," she said as she turned the steering wheel with all her might. Tin Lizzie bumped up over the grass bank and landed with a thud on a stony area.

"Whoa!" We both cried as the car tilted to the left, and we were up on two wheels. My nose was squashed up against the window, then I landed on Emma's lap as all four wheels hit the ground with a thud.

"Get off me, Rusty!" she shouted, elbowing me back to my seat.

I shouted back, "Stop the car, Emma! I need to get out."

"I'm trying to stop the car, but nothing is happening. I think my shoe is stuck on the accelerator pedal!" she cried as she wrestled with the steering wheel to keep us upright. "Oh, no! This is a very steep hill. I can't stop this pesky car, Rusty. Hold on tight."

"With what?" I yelled back. "I only have paws."

Lizzie bounced and bumped, going faster and faster as we hurtled down the hill. She banged and shuddered, shook and rattled, sending the squawking parrot over my head to the back seat. Emma's hat flew off her head and landed on mine. I tumbled on to the floor then bounced back on to the seat.

Emma's knuckles turned white, as she used all her strength to keep hold of the steering wheel. She bounced higher and higher on the springy mattress seat, banging her head repeatedly.

Mr. Musk continually squawked, "Hold on tight!" from somewhere in the car.

Emma suddenly screamed out "Oh, no, no, no!" as we went into a huge *bramble bush.*

It felt like we hit a rubber wall. Now the car was shooting backwards and forwards, as if it was tied to a piece of elastic. The car then shuddered, spluttered, hissed, and banged before grinding to a halt.

I opened my eyes. I was now lying upside down on the back seat. I quickly counted my four legs, relieved I still had them.

I could see Emma's driving shoes sticking out of the window, entwined in brambles. Emma was still attached to them, laying down across both front seats. The parrot was nesting in the feathers on top of Emma's hat which was in the footwell.

Emma pulled herself up breathing heavily and asked, "Oh, Rusty, Mr. Musk, are you all right?"

"Well, I'm not hurt, Emma, but I will probably need therapy after this experience," I snapped.

"Probably need therapy! Probably need therapy! Stop the car!" echoed Mr. Musk.

CHAPTER 18

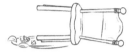

No, Emma! No!

"OUCH! That stings!" I yelped, as Emma dabbed my paw with one of her magic potions.

"That was a big thorn, Rusty. It had to come out." She dabbed the potion onto her forehead, where an enormous red lump had formed. "I'm sure it will make this better, too."

"At least we're all in one piece," she said, putting my dinner into my bowl. "Poor *Tin Lizzie*," she sighed "I really didn't want to leave her in the bramble bush."

I looked up at her. "Well, I hope you're satisfied, Emma. What a mess. I told you it was a stupid idea, driving your car. You are now a child and the sooner you start acting like one, the safer we will be."

"I guess you are right, Rusty," she said as she moved a kitchen chair in front of a tall cupboard. Climbing onto it, holding a long wooden spoon, she sniffled and grumbled "Hmmm, act my age, whatever that is."

"Now what are you doing?" I asked, not quite believing my eyes, as she started to poke the wooden spoon at a large bottle on the top shelf.

"It's my homemade elderflower elixir, and I want to drink a glass of it," she huffed as she prodded at the bottle with the spoon. "It's a very good tonic and calms the nerves."

"EMMA!" I growled. "You haven't listened to a single word I said, have you? Oh, for goodness sake, Emma, you do not need a tonic. Elixir is very good for old people. You are a child. Actually, I will correct that last statement. Your body is a child's and it's pure and without any nasty toxins, and it's still growing. As for your brain, well that's a whole different ball game."

Emma peered down at me with one of those looks that says, "you're right, and I hate you."'

Just then, the rickety chair began to wobble, and as she tried to steady herself, her hand holding the spoon caught the side of the bottle. I watched with my mouth open as the bottle of elderflower elixir slowly tumbled from the shelf onto the top her head. Emma's eyes crossed and rolled back as she fell off the chair on to the floor.

Mr. Musk appeared, screeching "I hate you! I hate you!" over and over, as he perched on the table, head bopping and his beady eyes fixed firmly on me.

"Oh, Emma! Emma, are you ok?" I asked as I nuzzled her neck.

"Err, um, what happened Wusty?" she murmured opening one eye. " I wuv ooh and I wuv Mr. Musky."

"Thank you, Emma. I'm so happy you are OK!" I replied as I vigorously licked her nose and cheeks.

"Err, stop it, you know I don't like that," she blurted, pushing me away.

"I wuv ooh! I wuv ooh! Stop it! Stop it! Don't like that!" interrupted the parrot.

Emma sat up and rubbed the top of her head. "Ouch, that hurt. I think I've got another bump, and my face is covered in dog slobber. What happened, Rusty?"

"Slobber! Slobber! Wuv ooh! Don't like it!" continued the bird as he ran frantically around in circles on the table. "Slobber! Stop it! Stop Slobbering! Wuv Rusty! Ooh! Another bump! Another bump!"

"If you shut that pesky parrot up, I'll tell you, Emma." I growled, climbing into my basket, feeling a little upset after having been pushed away for slobbering. I mean, what else could I do? I could hardly make her a cup of tea.

Emma coaxed the noisy bird into his cage with a slice of apple, shut the door and placed the blanket carefully over the cage. Peace at last. Then, sitting down next to my basket she said "I'm so sorry, Rusty. I know you're completely right. You're such a wise old puppy. I've been acting very foolishly and irresponsibly. Thank you for stopping me from drinking the elixir. How stupid of me! I know everything you said is true. I don't need the tonics now. I love my new young, wrinkle-free, ache-free, agile new me. I just forget sometimes, because in my mind I'm still ninety-year-old Emma. It's all so weird and wonderful."

Emma picked me up and sat down in her old armchair with me on her lap. She softly stroked my ears and asked, "Why do dogs slobber?"

"We don't slobber, as you call it. We are kissing you, telling you we love you, and we care." I said looking up at her. "When we're happy and excited, we wag our tails, but believe me, that is quite exhausting sometimes, and to my knowledge, apart from me, dogs cannot talk, so we believe that a good 'slobbering' as you describe it, is the only way to say 'I love you.'"

"I love you too, Rusty." murmured Emma, closing her eyes as we both fell soundly asleep.

CHAPTER 19

Where Is Old Emma Puff?

"*E*mma! Emma!" shouted George, shaking her shoulders. "Emma, wake up."

George arrived early this morning carrying a big bunch of flowers and after calling out for Emma several times and getting no response he frantically searched the cottage.

"Good Lord," he mumbled to himself as he nearly tripped over the unopened bottle of elderflower elixir that lay on the kitchen floor. "Emma, wake up!"

She opened her eyes. I could tell that the shock of seeing George's red face and runny nose almost touching hers came as a massive shock, as she immediately sat bolt upright.

"Morning, George." she said with the biggest smile.

George wiped his nose with the grubby handkerchief and asked, "Whatever has been going on Emma and where's your aunt? 'Cause she is not in her bed. I looked already and it not even been slept in!"

"Hah" I said, from under the table. "Now what are you going to tell him?"

"Oh, isn't she? Are you sure?" quizzed Emma as she made her way to the kitchen sink tap and filled a glass with water.

"Of course, I'm sure. I might be old, but I'm not stupid." retorted George.

"Erm, she felt better and said she had to go out. Said she wouldn't be long, and, erm, I must've fallen asleep in the armchair, waiting for her to come back."

"Right, then, well, she didn't come home!" said George grabbing his hat. "Stay right where you are. I won't be long," he urged, marching to the door.

"But, George," called Emma. "I have something very important to tell you."

The door slammed, and he was gone.

"Oh boy, he's so worried Emma. Were you finally going to tell him the truth?" I asked.

"Yes, I wanted to tell him everything. He's been such a good friend to me for many, many years, but now I won't get a chance to, because he's gone to get the police."

Emma picked me up. "I guess this is it, Rusty," she sighed. "We are now officially missing, well, the old versions of Emma Puff and Rusty are. I guess I couldn't keep pretending that I was out or unwell, could I?"

"No, Emma, you certainly could not. I wonder what will happen to us now?" I sighed.

"*Out! Unwell! Guess this is it!*" repeated Mr. Musk, but not from the curtain pole. He had taken a fancy to Emma's hat and spent most of his time sitting on top of the hat stand, constantly cooing to the feathers.

"Emma, dear." said George, as he stepped into the kitchen with a man following him. Putting his arm around her, he said "This is Police Constable Stubbs. Come and sit down at the table with him and I'll make us all a nice cup of tea." He smiled at Emma. "Nothing to worry about my dear, we think your Aunt Emma may have got lost. Policeman Stubbs needs to ask you some questions so we can find her."

Emma sat down at the table, I jumped onto her lap.

Officer Stubbs, a large jolly man, who'd been the local policeman for as long as I could remember, took a notebook from his pocket, sat down next to us and asked,

"When did you last see your aunt?"

CHAPTER 20

Policemen Everywhere

*G*eorge had been making pots of tea all morning. I think this is his fourth pot. A lot of different policemen had been in and out of the cottage. I heard them say that the whole village had joined in the search for Emma Puff.

Policeman Stubbs came back into the kitchen and announced, "We've found Emma's old car at the bottom of that steep hill that runs down from Whipps Farm. Looks like it crashed into a bramble bush. Not much damage, but no sign of Emma."

Looking at Emma, George asked, "So she went out in her old car, Tin Lizzie?"

"I didn't know she had a car," Emma lied, meekly.

"She stopped driving that a good few years ago, when her eyesight got worse and it made her back ache," said George, wiping his nose and scratching his puzzled head.

"*Tin Lizzie! Tin Lizzie! Whaw!* Back *ache!*" squawked the parrot, before nestling down again with his new love.

Emma was getting fidgety, and I was bored. We both knew that all this fuss was a waste of time. Then George called out "Your friends are outside Emma. Go and see 'em. They're asking 'bout you."

We ran up the path and were greeted with Sasha holding her arms out, "Good grief, Emma, this is awful." The three boys joined in a group hug.

No one cuddled me!

"Thank you, but I'm fine, honestly." smiled Emma. "Please don't worry. The police are sure she'll turn up eventually. My aunt does strange things sometimes, and if she doesn't turn up, I'm sure she'll be out there somewhere having a big new adventure!"

"So, what's gonna happen to you now?" asked Spike. "They won't let you stay here all by yourself."

"Will they send you back to your grandfather?" asked Sasha.

"They are trying to call my, erm, grandfather, but erm, they, erm can't seem to reach him," Emma said. "They said a lady from social services will be taking me to a nice family who lives nearby until they can, erm, reach him or, erm, find my aunt," said Emma "And I can take Rusty."

"So, does that mean you will still come to our school after Christmas?" asked Leroy.

"And we can still all play together?" added Specs.

"I'm sure it does," replied Emma. "You're my best friends, and no one is going to keep us apart because we have so much fun together."

"What about Mr. Musk? Can you take him too?" asked Specs. "He's the best parrot in the world."

"With the worst language!" laughed Emma. "You three boys saw to that."

"Did he say all that stuff we taught him?" laughed Spike.

"He certainly did, and to a lot of people," giggled Emma.

She then told them all about Mr. Musk's conversations and with whom. Shrieks of laughter bellowed out.

"Mr. Musk is going with my aunt's friend George for now. He knows George and social services did say they would ask if he could come with me later. I guess it depends on how the people I'm going to stay with feel about having a noisy parrot in their home."

"Well, at least you can keep this little fella," said Leroy, cuddling me close and stroking my ears.

"Did any of you get into trouble with your mums when you got home with all the goo all over you?" asked Emma.

"Nah," said Spike. "We all told the truth, and you were right. Every one of our mums ended up in tears of laughter and admitted that they would have loved a fun food fight, too. My mum just told me not to dare try it at home."

Just then a small black car stopped in front of the cottage. We all watched silently as a lady wearing blue jeans and a bright orange jacket with fringes on it stepped out of the car. She had long black hair woven with beads of all colours and big brown eyes. She looked over and beamed a big smile at us then opened the boot of the car, took from it a large green folder, and walked quickly up the path to the cottage. George opened the door, ushered her in, and called out "Emma dear, come in now, please!"

CHAPTER 21

Time to Say Goodbye

"Emma dear, this is Miss Allgood. She's here to help you," said George.

"Hello, Emma. I'm Lucy Allgood. You can call me Lucy." she said with a big smile. "Come and sit down with me, and I'll explain what's going to happen until we find your aunt or are able to reach your grandfather."

Holding Emma's hand and leading her into the living room, she said, "Hey, don't look so worried, you'll be fine." Then, looking at me, she said, "You're adorable!" and tickled my chin.

I liked her. And she smelt really nice. She had a painted face, just like those women in the bank. I curled up and listened to every word.

"I'm going to take you and this little fella to a very nice couple called Tom and Gemma Goldheart. They live in a fabulous house with a big garden not far from here, and you will still be able to see your friends." she smiled. "They know all about you and have already said to me that you can have your friends over anytime. I am guessing they are the ones that are outside?"

"Yes, they are really nice and want me to go to their school." replied Emma.

"I can arrange that, no problem," said Lucy Allgood, checking through her green folder. "School's out now for Christmas, so hopefully we will get you in after the holidays."

She stood up. "You're going to have an amazing Christmas, Emma, and I promise you the Goldhearts are lovely and have lots of fun. None of the children that stay with them ever want to leave! "

"Hah," I said. "We'll be there forever then."

Emma glared at me.

"Now go and pack up all your things, Emma, and if you need help, just call me." she said as she started to make a fuss of me.

George stood on the doorstep holding Mr. Musk's cage. He had it covered to keep the parrot quiet. Emma handed him her old hat. "He loves this hat, George. I think it's the feathers, or it reminds him of my aunt. I'm going to miss him so much."

"Don't you worry 'bout this 'ere silly old parrot, my dear," he said, taking the hat. "That nice lady said he'll probably be able to join you very soon, and if not, he will be fine with me. Keep me company, he will, 'til that aunt of yours gets back."

Then he wiped his runny nose with the grubby handkerchief, walked up the path, and opened the car door so Emma and I could climb inside.

"You be good, both of you, and I'll see you soon," he said as he shut the door.

Miss Allgood said goodbye and started to drive off.

"Stop the car, stop the car!" screeched Emma. "I've forgotten something and it's very important."

"All right dear, calm down," said Miss Allgood as she hit the brakes.

Emma jumped out of the car and ran up the road as fast as she could, and I was right behind her. "George! George!" she hollered. "George, wait."

George stopped and turned around to see Emma waving her arms and jumping up and down.

"It's important. Come back," she pleaded. "Please!"

I asked, "What's the matter? What's going on?"

"Shush, Rusty, not now, I have to do this," she replied.

Huffing and puffing, George made his way back to the cottage.

"Give me the key," demanded Emma. "Give it to me now. I've forgotten something important."

George reached into his pocket, pulled out the big old key, and handed it to Emma.

She ran to the cottage and disappeared inside, only to reappear moments later. Emma locked the door and ran back to George. She handed him the key and also a small bottle of medicine, then looking up into his eyes, she said, "Listen to me, George. This is very important. Aunt Emma wants you to take this for your knees. It will make them better and she said you are to take it tonight, before you go to bed."

Then Emma ran back down the road. I followed and we jumped back into the car. Miss Allgood smiled at Emma and asked, "OK?"

Emma wiped a tear from her eye with her sleeve and nodded a silent "yes."

CHAPTER 22

The Wonderful Goldhearts

*M*iss Allgood stopped the car in front of a pair of huge wrought iron gates. She opened her window and stretched out her arm and pressed a bright shiny button on the wall.

And then, as if by magic, the wall said, "Hello, who's calling?"

Whoa, this is some sort of witchcraft. I jumped onto Emma's lap and said, "Did you see that? The wall can talk."

"It's all right, Rusty. Everything is fine," she whispered and stroked my ears.

Then Miss Allgood spoke back to wall and said her name and the huge gates slowly swung open without anyone pushing them.

"Are you sure, because those gates are opening by themselves."

"Yes, I'm sure, Rusty," Emma laughed.

We drove up a long driveway with trees on either side and then the smartest house I'd ever seen was standing in front of us. It was painted white with lots of windows and shutters on each one.

Lots of green plants were climbing up the walls, some with big red roses. Its roof was red and had several tall chimney pots with streams of long swirly grey smoke coming out of them, disappearing into the blue sky above.

Steps led up to the front porch, where two large marble columns stood on either side of a massive wooden door supporting the canopy above.

The door opened wide and a tall man with wavy black hair, wearing blue jeans and a white sweater, and a woman with a lot of curly red hair, also wearing blue jeans with a black sweater, stepped out onto the porch.

"Wow," gasped Emma, with her nose pressed up against the car window. "This place is amazing."

Miss Allgood smiled at Emma, opened her door and said "Yes, it is. You and Rusty are going to love living here with Tom and Gemma Goldheart. They are the nicest people I know." Then, opening Emma's door, she said "Come on, let me introduce you."

I was first out of the car and headed for the nearest tree.

"Wow, look at this garden, Emma. It's huge!" I shouted as loud as I could.

CHAPTER 23

Christmas Is Coming

$\mathcal{M}$y tail was aching. I've never wagged it so much. Everything in this house is so cool.

Tom and Gemma Goldheart welcomed Emma with open arms. They fussed and cuddled me nonstop.

They are a youngish couple. I have no idea how old they are, but they don't have any of those lines or cracks on their faces, and their eyes sparkle.

I also had no idea how long it had been since Emma and I had become young overnight. The only clue I had was that Christmas music was playing all over the house, and Tom and Gemma were singing along with some of the songs.

Emma unpacked her bags. She quietly stood looking at the beautiful bedroom that was to be hers for as long as she stayed.

"No leaky roof to deal with here, Emma, and just look at your fancy bed." The bed was tall with posts that reached to the ceiling with pink drapes. It was fit for a princess. "It's so big and soft," I said as I sniffed around the room. "What do you think so far?"

"Everything is wonderful. Tom and Gemma are so kind, and I have never seen such a beautiful house as this one. I'm a bit nervous

because they keep saying to me 'Sing along with us, Emma, and show us your moves' when they start dancing. I've never heard any of that music before. When they dance about, they look like they have ants in their pants."

Emma sat down heavily on the bed. "The last time I danced it was a waltz, and the last song I knew all the words to was Vera Lyn singing 'We'll Meet Again' and that was during the Second World War."

I looked up into her eyes. "Well, Emma Puff, you'd better learn some then. Over on the table are loads of magazines, with pictures of young people on them. It doesn't matter whether you're eight, nine, ten, eleven or twelve years old. You've got to get with it."

"Emma?" called Tom, from the bottom of the stairs. "Come and help with the Christmas tree. We are going to decorate it."

"Oh, my goodness," gasped Emma looking up at the tree. "That is the biggest Christmas tree I have ever seen."

"Yep, she's a biggie," laughed Gemma. "And look, glitzy stuff." She said, pointing to some boxes. "Baubles, ribbons, every colour and size, you name it, it's in there."

Tom came into the room carrying a ladder on his shoulder and a big reel of fairy lights.

"Let's get this party started!" he said, turning up the volume to the music that seemed to be coming out of every wall. He started singing along to "Santa Claus Is Coming to Town" as he climbed the ladder with the lights, "He knows if you've been bad or good, so be good for goodness sake."

The tree looked amazing, and we all sat down and admired it. Tom gave me a doggy treat and the biggest fluffiest new bed ever. "Come on, little fella." he said pointing to it. He didn't have to ask twice. I threw myself headfirst into a cloud of deep soft snugly warmth.

Gemma put a large tray of goodies onto the coffee table. "Help yourself, Emma." she said, offering her a plate. "We hope you like your room. Do you need anything else honey bunny? We understand you've had a lot to deal with, so don't be shy. Just ask. We're here for you."

"I love my room and the bed is so pretty I think I should sleep on the floor because I don't want to spoil it," said Emma, helping herself to a mince pie. "You are both so kind, thank you for having us here. But there is something I need help with." she said coyly, looking at Gemma.

Gemma put her arm around Emma's shoulders. "Just ask, honey bunny. Your wish will be granted."

"Well, erm," started Emma, "my grandfather, whom I lived with before coming to my aunt, was very strict with me and well, erm..." she hesitated.

"Will you teach me to dance, please?"

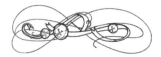

CHAPTER 24

Snow-Covered Boots

I've been talking all night to you, and now it's Christmas morning. I can hear Emma coming down the stairs.

Slowly the double doors opened, Emma stepped silently into the room wearing her fluffy blue pyjamas, her eyes wide with excitement as she surveyed the scene before her.

She gasped, "Oh wow, just look at those gifts under the tree!" Picking me up, she said, "Happy Christmas, Rusty." Then she squeezed me tightly.

When Emma opened the curtains she beamed. Her face glowed with the biggest smile as she stared at the huge white fluffy snowflakes gently tumbling from the wintery sky. "Merry Christmas, Emma." I whispered into her ear.

"HO, HO, HO," said Gemma and Tom in unison as they entered the room wearing giant Santa hats with silver bells draped around their necks while doing a silly jig. They started singing,

"Merry Christmas to you.
Reindeer poo on your shoe.
If you've been naughty,
No presents for you."

Emma put me down and I dove into my bed. This was crazy stuff.

"Oh, Merry Christmas to you two, too," Emma said, laughing as she threw her arms around Tom and Gemma. "Thank you so much for looking after Rusty and me. You're both amazing and very funny." Then, she pointed to the window, barely containing her excitement, and said, "Best of all, It's snowing, it's Christmas morning, and it's all just so perfect."

Tom scooped me up into his arms and said, "Merry Christmas, little fella." In return, I gave him a big slobbering lick. He didn't squeal or push me away. He didn't mind at all. He just laughed and ruffled my ears. We are definitely best buddies.

He then pulled a huge, juicy bone with a large silver bow tied around it from a hiding place. He slipped the bow around my neck as he gently put me down. "Rusty, here's a special treat for you. Enjoy." The bone smelt delicious, but wearing a silver ribbon around my neck didn't do it for me — but hey, it's Christmas.

Gemma and Emma were on their knees looking at the beautifully wrapped gifts under the tree. They examined each package one by one, gently shaking them trying to guess what they might contain. "They're all so pretty, I don't want to open them," said Emma with a dreamy sigh as she held up a box covered with multi-coloured ribbons that curled and twirled.

Tom was standing next to a table pointing to a large dome shaped parcel that practically took up the whole tabletop. "Well, you have to come here and open this one.

It's got your name on it, Emma," he announced.

"Oh wow, this is exciting! Whatever can it be?" exclaimed Emma.

"Open it." said Tom and Gemma in unison.

This was one of those times when you get that feeling in your tummy that something good or bad is about to happen. I pricked up my ears and carried on enjoying my bone, keeping both eyes fixed on the dome-shaped gift.

Emma climbed onto a chair and removed the big red bow from the top of the wrapping, then she carefully pulled the wrap off to reveal Mr. Musk sitting on top of her old red feathered hat. He opened his beady eyes and took his head out from under his wing, shook his bright blue feathers and squawked,

"Ho Ho Ho. Donner and Dancer! Stop pooping when you are flying!

Ho Ho Ho. It's hitting my hat! Naughty or nice! Merry Christmas! Ho Ho Ho. Pooping! Flying! Merry Christmas!"

Everyone burst into laughter.

Emma gasped "Mr. Musk, Mr. Musk." and opened his cage door. Mr. Musk hopped onto Emma's arm and up onto her shoulder.

A feeling of gloom rushed through me, and I leapt from my bed and ran to the table, hoping this was a bad dream. I stared up at the feathered creature bobbing his head and taking in his new surroundings.

He peered down at me with his beady eyes. I could have sworn that he grinned, but that would be ridiculous. Then to my horror he landed on top of my head, pooped, and squawked, "Don't poop when you're flying! Ho Ho Ho! Merry Christmas!" Mr. Musk immediately returned to Emma's shoulder.

The pesky parrot was back. My tail drooped between my legs. I slowly walked back to my bed, I climbed into it and closed my eyes and covered my ears with my paws. But with my keen hearing, that wasn't enough to muffle the sound of a car coming up the drive.

"Emma, honey," said Gemma, as she looked out of the window and saw the car. "Last night Miss Allgood called us about a young boy, who like you, has no family. He was found wandering around in the cold. Miss Allgood took him home with her last night. We' invited him to join us for Christmas or maybe longer. I think they just arrived."

This sounded interesting. I immediately scrambled from my bed and dashed to the front door, my tail now furiously wagging with excitement and curiosity.

Tom took hold of Emma's hand, and they followed Gemma to the large wooden front door, which Gemma opened wide. Flurries of snowflakes blew onto my face and tickled my nose.

Standing on the front porch just behind Miss Allgood was a very nervous-looking young boy.

Emma looked at his snow-covered boots, muddy trousers, and scruffy oversized jacket. Suddenly, I could tell Emma's heart had skipped a beat, and I could see the goosebumps on her arms as she watched the boy pull from his pocket a large, grubby handkerchief and wipe his runny nose.

"Emma, honey," said Gemma. "I'd like you to meet George Cracknall."

THE END.

GLOSSARY

Biscuits (noun)
Cookies

Bloomers (noun)
An old-fashioned piece of women's underwear like long, loose underpants.

Bonnet (noun)
The hood of a car, that covers the engine.

Bramble bush (noun)
A rough, prickly shrub with sharp thorns.

Bum (noun)
The part of your body you sit on. Can also be called backside, butt, bottom, or behind.

Dollop (noun)
A small amount of food that falls off a spoon, like a *dollop of whipped cream.*

Elixir (noun)
A liquid with magical powers to cure something.

Fairy lights (noun)
Christmas lights.

Fiddle-faddle (exclamation)
Something that is nonsense or not important.

Fiddlesticks (exclamation)
An old-fashioned word used to express disappointment or frustration.

Fizzy pop (noun)
A drink with bubbles in it, like a cola or soda.

Jumble Sale (noun)
A sale with cheap second-hand items. Also called a rummage or yard sale.

Lorry (noun)
A truck.

Mince Pie (noun)
A Christmas dessert filled with mincemeat which is made up of fruit, spices, and suet.

Mum (noun)
Mother.

Piddle (verb)
Peeing or urinating.

Plonking (verb)

Setting something down heavily, carelessly or casually.

Sphere (noun)

A round ball.

Podgy (adjective)

Someone or a body part that is short and chubby.

Poppycock (exclamation)

Nonsense.

Pound Sterling (noun)

British money.

Pyjamas (noun)

Pajamas or clothes for bed.

Social Services (noun)

The local or government agency that helps older people, orphans, sick people, and others.

Specs (noun)

A shortened version of the word spectacles which are eyeglasses.

Tablets (noun)

Pills.

Tea (noun)

A drink made by pouring boiling water over tea leaves.

In the United Kingdom, it can also refer to a small afternoon or early evening meal with small sandwiches, biscuits, and tea to drink.

Tin Lizzie (noun)

A name given to a very old car, usually an antique Ford from the early 20th century.

Trainers (noun)

Sneakers or tennis shoes.

Trifle (noun

A cold dessert made of cake and fruit with layers of jelly, custard, and cream.

Trivet (noun)

A small plate that is placed under a hot dish to protect a table.

Tyre (noun)

Tyre or wheel on a car.

Welly boot (noun)

Waterproof boots that are especially good for wearing in wet or muddy places "Wellies" got their name from their inventor, Arthur

Wellesley, the first Duke of
Wellington.

Wool (noun)

Heavy or thick thread or
fabric sometimes made from
sheep's wool.

EMMA PUFF'S SECRETS BOOK CLUB QUESTIONS

Who saved Rusty when he was a puppy the first time?

1: The fairies

2: A policeman

3: George Cracknall

What lie did Emma tell the other children about what had happened to her clothes?

1: She ate them.

2: She left them on the train.

3: She threw them away.

Why was Leroy so upset after playing on the tyre swing?

1: He lost his baseball cap.

2: He lost his sweets.

3: He lost his shoes.

What keeps Mr. Musk quiet at night time?

1: Music

2: A red blanket

3: A book

What is the name of Emma's car?

1: Tin Can

2: Tin Soldier

3: Tin Lizzy

How did Emma make her driving shoes?

1: With paper and string

2: Sticking rubber soles together

3: She bought them in a shop

What does Emma use to start her car?

1: A crank

2: A key

3: A banana

Who went shopping with Emma?

1: Rusty and George

2: Rusty and Sacha

3: Spike and Specs

What did Spike, Specs and Leroy teach Mr. Musk?

1: The alphabet

2: How to drive

3: Naughty words

How old is Emma Puff?

1: 25

2: 90

3: 5

Who is Emma pretending to be?

1: Her own great niece

2: Her own sister

3: Her best friend

What is the name of the social worker?

1: Miss Nice

2: Miss Lovely

3: Miss Allgood

Who shocked Mr. Doshmore, the bank manager?

1: A giant

2: Mr. Musk

3: Mrs. Doshmore

Who can hear Rusty talking?

1: Everyone

2: Mr. Musk

3: Emma Puff

Would you enjoy being naughty and having a food fight?

1: Yes

2: Yes

3: Yes

Why are there no curtains hanging from Emma's curtain pole?

1: She uses blinds.

2: She has no windows.

3: Parrot poop.

What happened to make Emma and Rusty young?

1: Anti-ageing cream

2: Plastic surgery

3: Purple globes

What did Mr. Musk say on Christmas morning?

1: Happy Easter

2: Happy Birthday

3: Ho Ho Ho

What did Emma give to George when she said goodbye?

1: Her driving shoes

2: A horse

3: A bottle of her magic potion

What happened to make Emma crash her car?

1: She wasn't paying attention.

2: She saw George up ahead.

3: Her driving shoes got stuck.

Why do some dogs slobber?

1: Because they eat too much.

2: They love you.

3: They have no teeth.

Who is your favorite character and why?

Would you like to know what happens next?

To be the first to know when the next book will be available, join **Emma Puff's Secret Book Club** by signing up here: TK WHERE

ABOUT THE AUTHOR

Annie Wilde was born in London, England. As a young girl, she relocated with her family to the wilds of the Suffolk countryside. At sweet sixteen, she moved back to the big city to train as a hairdresser. It was the Swinging Sixties in London, and she was slap bang in the middle of all the excitement.

Since then, Annie's life has been full of twists and turns, back roads, main roads, highways, and junctions...all eventually leading to retirement on the Italian island of Sicily.

Upon sorting through a lifetime of memorabilia stored in her garage, she stumbled upon a box of stories and drawings that were from a time of bedtime story telling with her three children and four grandchildren. So, she decided to develop some of the characters and create her first book.

Annie remains young at heart and loves to spend time with people of all ages and from all walks of life.

ABOUT THE ILLUSTRATOR

Beebe Hargrove is a freelance illustrator. Her professional work features a variety of projects and styles. She has designed t-shirts, architectural illustrations, and several seasons of fine and fashion jewelry. She is proud of a series of murals she created collaboratively with her hometown and the non-profit King City In Bloom. Placed throughout the city on local businesses they tell the story of the town's inception and the people that planted its seeds. Always a fan of fantastic stories this collaboration with Annie Wilde on Emma Puff has been a joy. Annie's sense of big color, mess and fun has been a perfect fit for Beebe's love of strong lines and splashing paint. She studied Illustration at Cal State Fullerton and currently lives in Atlanta, Georgia, with her family and two precocious cats. She loves reading, exploring and supporting the arts wherever she finds it.

CPSIA information can be obtained
at www.ICGtesting.com
Printed in the USA
JSHW040823220723
45223JS00006B/38